'What do *yo*   drawled lazily.

'I——' Sam was in danger of kissing his neck, which was temptingly close. 'I don't know.'

'Yes, you do,' he whispered.

'Will you let me go?'

'Moving your hips against me like that is only likely to ensure that I won't,' he murmured, and Sam's eyes widened in shock as she felt his instant arousal against her.

Dear Reader

Well, summer is almost upon us. Time to think about holidays, perhaps? Where to go? What to do? And how to get everything you own into one suitcase! Wherever you decide to go, don't forget to pack plenty of Mills & Boon novels. This month's selection includes such exotic locations as Andalucía, Brazil and the Aegean Islands, so you can enjoy lots of holiday romance even if you stay at home!

The Editor

Sharon Kendrick was born in West London. Leaving school at sixteen to try a variety of jobs and see the world, she then trained as a nurse. In the best romantic tradition, she fell in love with and married a doctor. While expecting her second child, Sharon got down to writing her first romantic novel. She loves writing, and the fact that such enjoyable work fits in so well with her life.

Recent titles by the same author:

CRUEL ANGEL

SWEET MADNESS

BY
SHARON KENDRICK

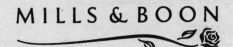

MILLS & BOON LIMITED
ETON HOUSE, 18-24 PARADISE ROAD
RICHMOND, SURREY TW9 1SR

To the world's greatest
living photographer—
Alastair McDavid, of Thistle.

*First published in Great Britain 1994
by Mills & Boon Limited*

© Sharon Kendrick 1994

*Australian copyright 1994
Philippine copyright 1994
This edition 1994*

ISBN 0 263 78513 0

*Set in Times Roman 10 on 12 pt.
01-9406-51283 C*

Made and printed in Great Britain

CHAPTER ONE

'*YOU!* You're Sam Gilbert?'

Sam swallowed, managing a smile. Of all the rotten luck—he'd remembered! 'Yes, I am. The name's deceptive, isn't it? I'm a Samantha, really. But I expect you thought you'd be interviewing a man, didn't you?' Now she was babbling.

His eyes, a dark, glittering blue, widened by a fraction—before returning to their shuttered narrowness; seeing all, telling nothing. 'Hardly,' he replied, his deep voice full of sarcasm. 'I wouldn't have read your c.v. if I thought that, and that kind of sloppy interview technique really isn't my style.' He paused. 'No, it isn't the name I'm thinking about.' He looked her up and down, experienced eyes flicking over her briefly. 'You're Charlotte Gilbert's sister,' he said slowly, and he made the simple statement sound as damning as an accusation.

Of course he hadn't forgotten; why should he have done? The faintest colour flared pink over Sam's cheeks as she recalled the other occasion when he'd seen her, just a week ago.

Charlotte had phoned, suggesting lunch. Well, not exactly *suggesting* lunch—demanding lunch would have been a more accurate description—but done in such a way, with an appeal to Sam's better nature, and the assurance that only Sam could help her work through her problems, that a refusal would have been not only churlish but impossible. 'You've *got* to see me, Sam,' Charlotte urged on the phone. 'I'm *desperate*!'

Sam's reluctance to see too much of her sister stemmed from the time when Charlotte had cold-heartedly run off with Sam's fiancé. Eight years on, tempers had cooled and Sam had forgiven, if not forgotten. And family was, after all, family. 'OK,' she agreed. 'Where shall we meet?'

'Luigi's.'

'*Much* too expensive,' said Sam firmly.

'Oh, *Sam*—don't be so dreary. Let's go there—it's fun. And I'll pay.'

'No, you won't—I'll pay for myself.'

One o'clock found Sam sitting at a table at the side of the room, waiting for Charlotte to arrive. The table was discreet and quiet, the kind of table she was always seated at, though Charlotte was the opposite. She always insisted on, and got, the centre-stage seat.

The waiter brought her a glass of fizzy water and a plateful of crudités and Sam sat munching and sipping until Charlotte breezed in.

She looked, thought Sam, absolutely wonderful—every inch the model she had once been. She was tall, leggy, elegantly boned, with china-blue eyes and the kind of long flaxen hair which Rapunzel would have given her eye-teeth for—all combined to make her a number-one head-turner. She was dressed in a white linen sleeveless mini-dress which showed off the smooth pale toffee colour of her tanned skin. Bare brown legs were finished off with soft white leather pumps.

Sam, who had come straight from the studio, was dressed in her habitual uniform of leggings and a top, both a deep charcoal-grey colour which didn't show the dirt, but which didn't actually do a lot for her under-stated looks, so unlike her sister's, of dark brown hair with eyes to match, set in a milky-pale complexion.

They ordered food—avocado salad then pasta for Sam while Charlotte opted for melon followed by a grilled Dover sole. 'I'm dieting,' she confided.

Much more weight loss and she'd fall through the slats in the chair, thought Sam, but said nothing.

'And wine—we must have wine!'

'Not for me,' protested Sam. 'I have to work this afternoon.'

'Well, I don't. Bring me the wine list, will you?' Charlotte gave the waiter a dazzling smile, and he sped off to obey her.

They ate their first courses while Charlotte slugged great gulps of wine and proceeded to tear the latest sen-sation of the modelling world apart. 'It almost makes me feel like starting up again,' she said moodily, taking another sip from her glass, the liquid leaving her lips shimmering.

Sam speared a curve of chicory. 'Well, you can't,' she said practically. 'You've got Flora to look after. And you still haven't told me why you wanted to see me so urgently today. What's the panic?'

'Bob is.' Charlotte drained the glass and had it refilled immediately.

'Bob?' It was, Sam reflected, almost amusing that Charlotte should be so insensitive as to ask Sam's advice about the man she had seduced away from her without compunction. 'What's wrong with him?'

'You mean apart from the fact that he's dull, stuffy, totally wrapped up in golf and takes me for granted?'

'You *did* marry him,' said Sam rather pointedly, but the remark went completely over Charlotte's head. She had almost finished the bottle and was now slurring her words slightly.

'I need someone who understands my needs,' she said dramatically. 'Someone who—my *God*! Look who's here!'

Sam cast a sideways glance then wished she hadn't because, just entering the restaurant, accompanied by a stunning redhead, was the man popularly coined 'the thinking woman's fantasy', Declan Hunt, the acclaimed photographer. The man who, having made a mint in the States, was back in London with his secretary to set up a brand-new photographic studio.

And the man who was interviewing Sam next week for the prestigious post of his assistant.

'It's Declan Hunt, isn't it?' she said, keeping her voice deliberately casual, as she observed Charlotte's eyes glittering avariciously, wishing that something, anything, could transport her a hundred miles away from here.

'*Mmm*,' said Charlotte lasciviously, running a pink tongue over frosted lips. 'Sure is. Wonder who the overblown Amazon with him is, though.'

Sam looked at her sister aghast. 'What a dreadful expression to use,' she objected in a whisper. 'And apart from anything else, it's completely inaccurate. The woman's an absolute stunner.'

She was, too, tall, with beautiful long limbs and a shapely, magnificent bosom. Her hair was naturally auburn by the look of it and it fell in thick waves past her shoulders. She was wearing a kind of Sherwood-green jerkin and trousers tucked into brown leather boots which made her look like a very sexy bandit indeed.

'Huh,' said Charlotte, and, taking a last swig, she rose unsteadily to her feet. 'Well, let's give her something to think about.'

'Charlotte—where the hell are you *going*?'

'To see my old friend and colleague, dear Declan.'

Sam watched in silent humiliation as Charlotte weaved her way over to their table and shrieked, 'Declan!' to the darkly tousle-haired man whose brief frown indicated to Sam that, for a moment, he couldn't remember her sister from Adam.

This was soon rectified by Charlotte, who reminded him in a voice loud enough for the whole restaurant to hear. And here Sam bent her head, scarlet with shame, as Charlotte threw her arms around his neck and clung to him like a limpet.

She saw him shoot an apologetic look over his shoulder at the redhead whom Charlotte had pointedly ignored, before disentangling Charlotte firmly and indicating with a polite glance at the table that he wished to proceed with his meal.

Unfortunately, that was not to be an end to it. Charlotte came back to her own table, obviously disgruntled, and hell-bent on re-establishing her reputation as a *femme fatale*. And it seemed that her intentions to discuss her marriage problems with Sam had flown right out of the window, since Bob was not mentioned by her again, and any attempt by Sam to reintroduce him into the conversation was firmly quashed. Instead, she flirted like mad with the men on the next table, before allowing the two braying merchant bankers with their striped shirts and gin-flushed faces to join them, bringing with them a bottle of champagne.

As their laughter grew louder and more uncontrolled, Sam looked up, aware of being caught up in the dazzle of a hauntingly bright stare, as blindingly mesmerising as the headlights of a car on a pitch-black night. There was a renewed wail of affected laughter from Charlotte and her conquests, and an unmistakably derisive twist appeared on the hard, cold mouth of Declan Hunt—before he turned away, bending his head to listen to the beautiful redhead who was whispering into his ear with an amused smile. And it wouldn't take three guesses to imagine what she was saying to him, thought Sam gloomily.

Her torment ended only when Bob, Charlotte's husband, appeared at the door of the restaurant, with Flora, their daughter. And while Charlotte went off to repair her lipstick in the powder-room, Sam hurried over to her niece to sweep her up in a bear-hug, and have lots of wet kisses pressed enthusiastically into her neck.

'You're so good with kids, Sam,' said Bob, a touch wistfully, when the small hairs on the back of her neck started prickling as she became instinctively aware that she was being stared at, and, once again, she raised her head to look in the direction of the man who stared, frozen in time as he surveyed her with a pair of puzzled blue eyes.

Sam came back to the present to find that the eyes which studied her now were not puzzled; anything but. They were faintly disapproving.

'So you're Charlotte Gilbert's sister,' he repeated.

'Yes. We don't look alike.' We *aren't* alike, she wanted to say, but you couldn't very well denigrate your sister to a total stranger.

'No, you don't.' The eyes held her in their thrall, piercing and direct, like twin blue swords.

That day in the restaurant, he had been wearing a dark and superbly cut suit with a dazzlingly white collar and a tie and, barring the thick and unruly waves of his dark hair that had stubbornly refused to lie flat, he had looked the epitome of elegant sophistication.

But today he looked different. Today, he was dressed from head to foot in denim, with the dark hair curling untidily over the collar of his denim shirt, and the blue of the material only emphasised the cold blueness of his eyes. The denim of his jeans was faded to a paler blue, the fabric stretched almost indecently over long, muscular thighs which seemed to go on forever... Today, he was worlds away from the man she had seen in the restaurant. Today, he looked earthy, an innate sexuality shimmering off that lean physique like a haze.

Sam gulped. 'About that day——' But he silenced her with a shake of his head, so that all those tangled curls moved with a life of their own.

'That day had little enough to commend it without raking it over any further,' he said coldly. 'Tell me, do you make a habit of going on long, boozy lunches and picking up total strangers? It could get you into all kinds of trouble.'

She half wanted to say, *I'm* not like that—*I* was sober! But something in his high-handed manner angered her. Why *should* she attempt to defend herself to him? He probably wouldn't give her the job now in any case. And, even though she had been embarrassed by Charlotte's behaviour at the time, now she perversely felt a sudden stirring of loyalty. Charlotte had been out of order, yes— but, from the disapproving expression on Declan Hunt's face, anyone would have thought that they had both stood up on a table and performed a striptease!

She stared at him, her dark brown eyes sparking with insurrection, wondering how he would terminate the interview, when she decided that she would not give him that pleasure. 'It's all right, Mr Hunt,' she told him, with an attempt to sound at her most reasonable. 'I quite understand that you probably don't want to consider me for the job now.'

The flamboyant swoop of one ebony brow curved up by a fraction. 'Oh? And why's that?'

'You obviously disapprove of how I conduct my social life——'

But he interrupted her, with a small humourless laugh. 'Do you really think,' he began, 'that I only ever employ people of whose lifestyles I approve?' He rubbed his neck at a bare piece of skin, visible through the top button being open, and she found herself noticing where the tanned column of his neck became shadowed with dark whorls of chest hair. 'If I did that, Ms Gilbert, I can assure you that I would be chronically understaffed.' He put his head a little to one side, and stared at her consideringly, as if lining up a shot for the camera. 'I must admit that I do have reservations about you—but the company you mix with isn't one of them.'

Robin, her current employer, had told her bluntly that he was a difficult man, and she had been prepared to overlook that, making allowances for his genius behind the camera—but the reality of his caustic tongue had her senses sizzling with indignation. 'What reservations?'

He gave the smallest shrug, and Sam was irritated with herself for noticing that even that slight movement drew attention to the breadth of his shoulders, giving definition to the interplay of muscle which rippled beneath. Again, she was caught in the crossfire of his gaze.

'Well, firstly—there's your size,' he commented.

'My *size*?' She stared at him in bewilderment, for the briefest second experiencing every woman's universal fear—that he was accusing her of being fat. 'What's wrong with my size?'

'You're very small,' he said lazily. 'Quite tiny, in fact.'

Sam unconsciously drew herself up to her full height and tossed her head back, so that the heavy bob of her mahogany hair swayed like a wheatfield in the wind. 'I'm five feet three inches,' she pointed out. 'That's hardly midget class.'

The rugged features remained unconvinced. 'And you probably only weigh around ninety-five pounds.'

She mentally crossed her fingers. Didn't they say that a woman was allowed to lie about her age and her weight? And if Declan Hunt had some kind of problem with petite women, then lie she would. After all, she *did* want the job—and she didn't want him thinking that she was some undersized weakling, although she had to admit that standing in front of a man who was so big, and broad, made her feel decidedly more fragile than usual. 'I'm a hundred and ten,' she lied. 'And my size surely has nothing to do with my ability to handle a camera. Right?'

'*Wrong*. And I'll be handling the camera mostly, not you. I need an assistant, not a partner—and certainly not a liability. Someone to carry my equipment—hump it up and down stairs, into cars, over fields. I do not want to spend valuable time when I could be assessing the light quality worrying that you're going to give yourself a hernia, or, even worse, to find that you simply can't hack it and manage to drop a load of valuable and very expensive equipment.'

More used now to the intensity of that stare, Sam met his gaze squarely. 'Try me,' she challenged.

There was a brief smile as he acknowledged the challenge, and the dark, tangled head was nodded in the direction of a large silver box. 'Carry that camera over to the other side of the studio.'

The studio was vast and the box weighed a ton, but she would have died sooner than let *him* know that, and besides—her slight looks were deceptive. The squash she played twice a week had strengthened her, so that her 'tiny' frame—as he had called it so disparagingly—was surprisingly strong without being in the least bit sturdy. With a serene smile she accomplished his instruction. 'How's that?' she questioned guilelessly.

He sat down on one of the two facing leather sofas, his long, denim-clad legs sprawled out in front of him, a careless movement of his hand indicating that she should sit opposite him. 'Well, that's reservation number one disposed of,' he conceded.

'And number two?'

He gave a small sigh. 'Much more fundamental, and not so easy to reconcile, I'm afraid.'

She felt as though she was wandering through Hampton Court Maze, trying to follow his thought processes. 'And it is?'

'That you're a woman.'

'*That I'm a woman*?' she repeated, slowly and deliberately, so that there could be no mistake, mentally composing a letter of complaint to the Equal Opportunities Commission.

'That's right.'

'You don't like women?'

For the first time, he laughed, and for the duration of that laugh all Sam's indignation fled. Because the effect of that laugh softened the hard angles and planes of his face into the kind of sensational, sexy look which would knock women down like ninepins, and momentarily did the same for Sam. She felt as if some invisible punch had hit her solar plexus, robbing her not just of oxygen, but of reason, too. And yet with some unerring sense of self-preservation, she didn't show the slightest glimpse of her reaction, merely set her face into disbelieving lines as she waited for his reply.

'On the contrary,' he drawled. 'I love women.'

And some! She acidly noted his use of the plural.

'Love them, that is,' he continued, 'except at work.'

Not trusting her instinctive response to such out-and-out chauvinism, she forced herself to adopt logic. 'But you work with models all day,' she pointed out, 'most of whom are women.'

'Different women, and in short bursts.'

'So what's wrong with one woman—constantly?'

'Every bachelor's nightmare,' he murmured, half to himself, before looking up, his fingers locked as if in prayer, his eyes watching her face very closely. 'Women are emotional creatures, Ms Gilbert, don't you agree? And they tend to let their emotions get in the way of their work. It's a fact of life—the way they're made.'

'Perhaps you could be a little more—explicit,' Sam spluttered incredulously.

'Sure.' The ecclesiastical attitude of his hands changed as he moved them behind him to rest his head on them. 'Tell a man he's made a mistake, and what does he do?

He *learns* from his mistake. Tell a woman the same thing, and what does she do?'

'I don't know, Mr Hunt, but I'm sure you're going to tell me.'

The firm lips gave a cool imitation of a smile. 'She usually bursts into tears. Do you deny that?'

She *could* understand some women crying, especially with a man like this around to provoke them. Frankly, if *she* were incarcerated with Mr Declan Hunt all day long, she might just consider taking out shares in Kleenex! Not that she *was* likely to be incarcerated with him. She was destined for the door, no doubt, but let her leave him believing her to be a cool cookie. She mimicked his cool smile with one of her own. 'Some women, perhaps, Mr Hunt. Not this one.'

Another cool smile. 'So you've been working for Robin Squires for—how long?'

'Nearly two years.'

'My ex-boss,' he observed, an indefinable note in his voice. 'Tell me why you want this job so much,' he said suddenly.

Did it show that much? she wondered. Was her hero-worship of this man's work so apparent? She looked into his eyes. They had fenced for the whole of the interview; she probably didn't stand a chance. She had lied about her weight and let him carry on thinking that she be-haved as outrageously as her sister, but she respected him enough as an artist to give him her reply from the heart.

'I want to work with you,' she said simply, 'because of your book—*The Innocents*.'

His eyes shuttered like the closing of a lens, and his features became stony-cold—as forbidding as if they had been hewn from granite. 'I don't do that kind of work any more,' he said, and there was a new, harsh note to his voice.

My, but he was touchy! She wondered what she had said that was so wrong, and struggled to make amends. 'No. I know. But you can. You're capable of it, and that's enough for me.' She was aware that she had raised her voice, speaking with all the zeal that his masterpiece of a book had inspired in her when it had first been published three years ago. That book had changed her life in a way. Because of it she had gone to work for Robin—she had wanted to learn from the man who had taught Declan. And now, today, she was here with a chance of working for the man himself—if she hadn't blown it.

There was a long silence she didn't dare to disturb.

Still resting his head in his hands, he had tipped back so that he was now looking at the ceiling. When he lowered his head to look at her and spoke again, the harshness had disappeared, the cool drawl returned.

'I'm a fashion photographer now, Ms Gilbert. No more, no less. If you're looking for something deeper, something more meaningful, then you can walk out of this door right now.'

She held her breath.

'If, on the other hand, you want to learn how to take good professional fashion shots, then I'm your man.'

This last flat statement none the less sounded so like every woman's fantasy about Declan Hunt that Sam's thoughts were thrown into such confusion and she thought she must have misheard him.

'Wh-at?'

He gave her a look which might almost have indicated that he was in danger of changing his mind, so Sam forced herself to ask as casually as she could manage, 'You're offering me the job as your assistant?'

He nodded. 'If you want it.'

Oh, she wanted it. No doubt about that; what puzzled her was why he wanted *her*. 'But why me, a woman, after all you said about women?'

He frowned, then leant forward to the black folder which was on the table in front of him. It was her portfolio. He took out a black and white photo and held it up.

'Because of this,' he said, then, possibly to temper what sounded like unconditional praise, proceeded to tear it to pieces. 'Oh, it's crude,' he amended, 'in terms of composition. It's over-exposed and poorly lit. And yet...'

'Yet?' she prompted, tentatively—marvelling how his whole demeanour had changed when he spoke about the photograph—his face suddenly mobile, a certain animation about him as he gestured with the fine-boned, long-fingered hands. As though he had lost himself in the picture.

'Like all good pictures, it tells a story.' He fixed her with a sudden swift searing look. 'An unusual story, and one which I can't work out.'

Sam had been snapping children at Flora's birthday party, capturing the extremes of children's behaviour— the joy, the tears and the tantrums—but Declan Hunt had picked on the portrait of Flora herself taken two years ago, when she was only five. She'd given that shy smile which so rarely lit up her face, but even while smiling there came across the rawly vulnerable streak which lay at the heart of the child.

'She's sad,' he said softly.

Sam's throat constricted. Was it that plain? Or only to him—with those eyes which had been trained to see through to the core of every subject? What child wouldn't be sad with parents constantly caught up in their own private war? 'A little sad, perhaps. I must have caught her on a bad day,' she lied baldly, aware that he was waiting for more, but she wasn't prepared to give him any more.

His eyes narrowed, as if exploring his own possible explanations for her reticence to expand on the subject. 'I should have asked if you have any outside commitments?' he probed. 'Anything which would prevent you from giving less than a hundred per cent to the job? My hours are more demanding than Robin's ever were.'

She looked at him, her dark eyes huge with query. 'Such as?'

'A husband and daughter?'

She looked down at the photograph of Flora he was still holding, then down at her hands, a quick movement which hid her eyes, and then it suddenly clicked what he had inferred. Dear heaven—he was referring to the incident at the restaurant the other day. She remembered holding Flora tight, hugging her against her chest and then looking up slowly, some sixth sense telling her that she was being watched, to find that intense blue gaze upon her. Did Declan imagine that Bob was *her* husband, Flora *her* child? Oh, the irony if he did—for he couldn't have been more wrong if he'd tried.

'Flora is my niece, Charlotte and Bob's child. Bob— the man you saw—is Charlotte's husband, not mine,' she stated, then gave him a determined smile. 'If you're offering me the job, Mr Hunt, I'd like to accept.'

'Declan, then. Welcome.' He held out a hand and she did the same, allowing him to enclose her own in his firm, warm grip, aware of some thrill of recognition striking deep within her as flesh met flesh, and her conventional thanks flew out of her head as she was rendered speechless by the impact.

Dear heaven, she remonstrated silently once more, as the dark blue eyes surveyed her with nothing more than curiosity, is this how much of a prude you've become, that a man's touch can threaten to knock you right off balance? It was a simple handshake, nothing more. A deal sealed. Say something quickly, before he changes his mind.

'Thanks—Declan.' Exit on dry wit, she thought, and smiled. 'And I do want to reassure you that I promise to sublimate all those unattractive feminine qualities which you find so incompatible with work.' Except that somehow sublimate seemed to be entirely the wrong word, for his eyebrows arched arrogantly as she uttered it.

'Take most of what I said with a pinch of salt, Sam.' There was a glint of unholy devilment in those sea-dark eyes. 'I'm not really such an out-and-out chauvinist— but I haven't the easiest manner in the world when I'm working. Just testing that you could cope with it.'

So his provocative comments had all been his own bizarre form of interview technique! Sam glowered, tempted to—what? Her pulses were singing with temper—surely it was temper?—and she waited for him to speak, because she wasn't sure she could trust herself to say anything that wasn't grossly insubordinate, when at that moment the telephone rang.

He picked it up, listened, smiled, said, 'Fran!' as though someone had just told him he'd won the national lottery. 'Just one minute,' he said, then put his hand over the receiver. 'Phone my secretary tomorrow. Start date—when? A fortnight?'

'A month.'

He shook his head. 'A fortnight. I'll see you then.' And he gave her a polite nod of dismissal, continuing his conversation with 'Fran'—whoever she was—the knockout redhead he'd been with in the restaurant probably, thought Sam with unwelcome resentment.

She left the studio, trying to walk normally across the vast floor area, which was difficult when she knew that those enigmatic eyes were watching her, wondering why she should not be feeling like whooping for joy that she'd just landed a job with one of the world's greatest photographers.

Because joy was too strong a word to describe her feelings. Too strong and too simple.

She'd never come out of a job interview like this before, as churned up inside as if someone had just put her through the wringer. But then she'd never met a man like Declan before.

A brilliant man who was so abrasive, so unsettling.

And sexy as hell.

CHAPTER TWO

'WHY didn't you *warn* me?' Sam swung round to face Robin accusingly, the large silver hooped earrings she wore swaying wildly, like swings in a bird-cage.

'Warn you about what?' asked Robin, mock-innocently, a grin on his face.

'*Him*! Declan Hunt. He's unbelievable.'

'I did warn you—I told you that he was a genius. And a bastard. I thought that three years of working in the States might have tamed him a little, but apparently not.'

Something in Robin's eyes prompted her next question. 'What's he like?'

He shrugged. 'Who really knows with Declan? He's an intensely private man. I gave him his first job, you know. It's funny—even at eighteen I knew that he had the talent to go right to the top, to outclass anyone else of his generation.' He smiled at her. 'So he's offered you the job, huh? And naturally you've accepted.'

Sam shrugged, knowing that she would never share with Declan Hunt the kind of easygoing working relationship she had with Robin. 'I'd be a fool not to, wouldn't I?'

'I don't think so, but then I'm biased, aren't I? I'd rather have you stay here, with me.'

Sam smiled at Robin Squires. Though at fifty he was around two decades older than Declan, he too wore the ubiquitous denim. His broad cockney accent was an affectation, since he came from one of England's most

aristocratic families, and it was this that set him apart—
since many clients were still impressed by someone who
not only took good pictures, but had a title, too.

She shook her head regretfully. 'Oh, if only I could—
anything for an easy life—but this girl's career is demanding to take off, and Declan Hunt provides the
world's best launching pad.' She frowned. 'He told me
that my being a woman worried him, that he finds them
emotional to work with.'

Robin looked at her quickly. 'He said that?' He picked
up an eyeglass to scan a whole sheet of tiny 'contact'
photographs, and remarked almost casually, 'You know
that Gita used to be his assistant?'

Sam opened her mouth, then shut it again. 'Gita?' she
verified. 'His assistant? *Your* Gita?'

Robin put down the eyeglass. 'There's only one Gita.'
He gave a kind of blank smile. 'Isn't there?'

Yes, indeed. Robin's exquisite Indian wife had been
the model of her decade, retiring much too early, according to the pundits.

Gita.

With those wide dark-brown-velvet eyes that a man
could lose himself in, silky skin the colour of milky
coffee, and long, aristocratic limbs. And as Lady Squires,
Robin's wife, she now had a different career—that of
society beauty. Her two homes were always being fea-
tured in magazine and newspaper articles. And no race
meeting was considered anything if Gita was not there,
wearing one of the millinery creations for which she was
famous.

These days she rarely ventured near Robin's studio,
and on the few occasions that Sam had met her she had
found her stunning, aloof—and very slightly terrifying.

Sam frowned. 'I had no idea that Gita did photography before she started modelling.'

'Why should you have known? It was way before your time, and it's not something that I particularly broadcast. Anyway, she wasn't his assistant for very long. Declan saw her potential, decided she was wasted behind the lens—he took some shots and the rest, as they say, is history. They became overnight successes, and never looked back. In the beginning, she wouldn't let anyone else photograph her, which only added to his, and her, mystique.' He shot her another glance. 'You knew that they were involved, didn't you? Emotionally, as well as professionally?' He spoke the words quickly as if to get them over with, like a child gulping down a particularly nasty dose of medicine.

Sam shook her head, surprised by the sudden, inexplicable lurching of her heart. 'No. No, I didn't.' She was curious to know more, and yet, at the same time, strangely reluctant to hear it. 'Was it—serious?'

Robin gave a laugh which sounded forced. 'Very. The beautiful couple with the world at their feet. They could have been the Taylor-Burton combination of the photographic world.'

'But I don't remember reading anything about it,' said Sam slowly.

'You wouldn't have done. Declan is a man who guards his privacy well. He managed to keep the affair out of the tabloids, much to Gita's chagrin. She is——' he gave a rueful smile '—a keen self-publicist.'

'So what happened between them?' Sam was bursting with a need to know, then realised that Robin might consider it prying. 'Unless you'd rather not talk about it?'

But he shook his head. 'Our hero became disillusioned with the glitzy world of glamour photography and decided to do something meaningful with his life. This caused fireworks with Gita. She wanted a man at *her* side, not on the other side of the world. She gave Declan an ultimatum, which basically boiled down to if he did go and work in a war zone then it was all over between them.'

'And he...?' asked Sam tentatively.

Robin laughed. 'Declan's not a man you can tame, or bribe. He went right ahead with his plan. Naturally, being Declan, he excelled at photo-journalism, too. As you know, he became something of a national hero, when his war photographs were taken up by news agencies all around the world and were credited with achieving peace negotiations, where everything else had failed.'

'And—Gita?' probed Sam hesitantly.

'Oh, Gita.' He paused. 'I'm afraid that the war lost him Gita, because while he was out getting shot at she decided to marry me.'

'But—*why*?' said Sam, without thinking, then saw his face and could have kicked herself. 'I'm sorry, Robin— I didn't mean——'

He shook his head. 'I had something which Gita wanted.'

'What do you mean?'

He laughed. 'Oh, come on, Sam! A title. She's an ambitious lady, is my beautiful Gita, and marriage to me meant instant entry into the English aristocracy.'

'But wasn't Declan your—friend?' she asked haltingly.

Robin gave a wry smile. 'In as much as anyone could be a friend to Declan. He isn't like other people. There's something that sets him apart. Even Gita said that. You

mean did I feel bad about stealing his girl?' He laughed
again, that same empty laugh. 'Oh, I didn't feel great
about it; I should have resisted, but Gita is a fairly irresistible lady. She wanted me, and what she wants she
usually gets.'

'And did Declan—I mean—do you still speak?'

Robin looked at her in surprise. 'Oh, Declan isn't a
man to bear a grudge. "The best man won" was what
he said at the time. But whether Gita would agree, now
that he's back, I'm not sure,' he finished in an under-
tone which Sam had to strain her ears to hear.

She set about making coffee for them both, still
puzzled by what Robin had let slip. Had he been implying that Gita was still carrying a torch for Declan?
And what of Declan's feelings for Gita?

Sam shook her head and sipped her coffee. It's none
of your business, Sam Gilbert, she told herself sternly,
as she went into the dark-room to develop a film.

She started work exactly a fortnight later. The journey
from her flat in Knightsbridge was not exactly long, or
arduous, but she took care to rise at least an hour earlier
than she needed, and caught the Tube to Declan's studio.

She had been back there just the once, when he had
given her a key, and introduced her to the one other
permanent member of his staff, and she had been amused
to note that his reservations about working with women
were backed up by fact, since his secretary-cum-
receptionist was a man! Michael Hargreaves was a couple
of years younger than his boss, well-spoken, and ex-
ceedingly polite—he probably had to be to compensate
for his boss's shortcomings she thought. He also, according to Declan, spoke four languages with ease, and

had a heftily impressive Classics degree from Oxford. So quite what he was doing in a rather dead-end job as secretary she couldn't imagine.

She had thought that she'd be there before Declan, but as she pushed the door open she was greeted by the sight of his undeniably attractive posterior, clad in clinging black denim, as he fiddled around with a maze of thick black wires on the floor, and she was startled by the tingling as the little hairs at the back of her neck prickled in response to him. For Sam, it was an entirely new and not very welcome sensation, this blatantly physical response to a man she neither really knew nor particularly liked.

'Get me a screwdriver from out of the tool-box, would you?' he ordered abruptly, without turning round.

He obviously didn't believe in the red-carpet treatment, she thought crossly, as she draped her satchel over the back of a light-stand. A 'Good morning, Sam—welcome to your new job' wouldn't have cost him much. 'Where is it?'

'Believe it or not, it's the large box in the corner, cunningly marked "tools",' he returned sarcastically.

She walked over to the tool-box, opened it, and extracted two screwdrivers which she thought would do. 'But "tools" could mean anything, don't you think?' she answered, matching his sarcasm, with a sudden need to show him that she could give as good as she could get. 'For all I know it could be where you keep your supply of beer.'

'Come over here,' he said, completely ignoring her last remark, and indicated the space next to him. 'I need you to hold this wire for me.'

She crouched down beside him, and took the wire he'd pointed at, aware suddenly, and almost painfully, of his closeness. He was so close that she could detect some faint scent of lemon—soap, probably; somehow she could not imagine a man like Declan Hunt splashing aftershave all over that impressively shaped neck. So close, in fact, that she could see a minute scar which traced a thin line down one cheek, and just below it his razor had just slightly nicked a tiny spot of blood at the curve of a jaw which was both strong and sensual. A newly shaved jaw, but one where the shadow of the new beard would shortly reappear. He looked, she thought, like the kind of man who would probably shave twice a day and still have a darkly shadowed jaw...

'Far be it from me to interrupt your little reverie...' he drawled.

To her horror, she realised that he had been speaking to her, and she hadn't heard a word of it. 'I'm so sorry,' she babbled quickly. 'I was miles away.'

'Hmm. Well, don't daydream on my time.'

'I won't.' Well, if he had noticed her gazing at him like a soppy puppy, at least he had the decency not to draw attention to it.

He rose to his feet, and she did the same, a sudden flare of excitement running through her involuntarily which made her cheeks grow hot as she noticed that he was subjecting her to a similar kind of scrutiny—the only difference being that he didn't look in the least bit puppy-like. His eyes were narrowed as they swept over her, his face indifferent.

'Wear something a little more suitable tomorrow, will you?' he said shortly.

Sam stared at him with what she considered righteous indignation, hoping that it might rid her of this crazy excitement. 'I beg your pardon?'

'You heard. I'd like you dressed in something more substantial tomorrow.'

She glared at him. She had dressed with care for her first day. Nothing over the top, but she had thought it perfect—a fine-knit dark-caramel-coloured sweater which went well with the dark mahogany of her bobbed hair, slim-fitting black leggings, and short black ankle boots. 'What's wrong with what I've got on?'

He smiled, but not with his eyes. 'What are you wearing underneath your sweater?'

'Wh-at?'

He shrugged. 'You wanted to know what was wrong with your attire, and I'm about to tell you. It happens to be a perfectly legitimate question.'

And a perfectly redundant one, she thought with mortification as she realised just what he meant, because her nipples were pushing hard and painfully through her flimsy bra against the thin material of her sweater, as visible as if she were freezing cold. Only here, in his studio, she wasn't the slightest bit cold, which left only one other and highly disturbing reason for their tingling tightness.

Their eyes met in silent acknowledgement of her unwitting response to him, hers smouldering with resentment at this unwelcome power he wielded, his coolly indifferent, as though such a reaction was par for the course, and certainly nothing to get excited about.

This kind of thing just doesn't happen to me, Sam thought desperately, as the colour flared in her cheeks, feeling more vulnerable than she'd done for years, knowing that her face was on the verge of crumpling; and perhaps he saw it, for he made a small terse exclamation of something that sounded like surprise underneath his breath.

'You know,' he mocked softly, 'for a woman who kicks up a storm with strange men in restaurants that's a pretty good imitation of a little maidenly embarrassment.'

He can think what he likes, she thought fiercely, her confusion vanishing as anger took over. 'You still haven't told me why what I'm wearing isn't suitable.'

He sighed, clearly bored with the conversation. 'It's simply that I do a lot more location work than Robin. You'll be outside a lot more. Those clothes are fine, but not for clambering up ladders and striding across muddy fields. So tomorrow, wear something else. Denim is the most practical. Thick sweaters. Oh, and——' his eyes skimmed her breasts with lazy amusement '—thermal vests might be a good idea, too.'

Why wouldn't he let up? Did he enjoy baiting all women like this? She couldn't imagine Gita putting up with such taunts, and in that instant she decided to try her own form of retaliation.

'I forgot to tell you that Robin said to send his regards. He was saying that he and . . . Gita haven't seen you for a long time. Not since before you went to America, I believe?' she asked with innocent interest.

The effect was instant, and his reaction both gratified and sickened her as she saw his mouth tighten into an aggressively arrogant line, a brief and indeterminable light flaring before his eyes slit into dull shards. And, interestingly, a pulse started to throb at the base of his throat. It seemed that, just as hers had done, his body too was now betraying him. He was suppressing it, but there was more emotion written on that harshly handsome face than she'd seen there before. And all inspired by Gita's name. He's still in love with her, she thought flatly. And he's back. No wonder Robin was looking so uneasy.

The dark blue eyes bored into her like steel drills. 'That's really nothing to do with you, is it?' he said in a cutting voice so designed to put her in her place that she flinched. He glanced pointedly at the clock on the wall. 'Do you think if we've dispensed with all the social niceties you could actually get down to doing some work? Or did Robin pay you to just stand around looking decorative?'

What was she *doing*? Answering him back, stirring up trouble—all designed to put his back up, and why? Just because she was angry with herself for reacting to him so powerfully? Bad start, Sam.

She decided to try to make amends. 'What would you like me to do, Declan?'

Declan looked as if he could quite happily have strangled her before firing her on the spot, thought Sam unhappily, though she doubted whether he'd be so lacking in circumspection as to leave himself in the lurch without a replacement.

'We've got a shoot this afternoon. You can start by tidying the dark-room and replenishing the solutions. After that you can check the lights and load up my 34mm and 2 and 1/4 sq cameras. And you'd better see whether we need any new backdrops—the rep's coming this afternoon. And when you've done all that you can make yourself some coffee. I'll be out for most of the morning—I want to check out a location. After that I'm having lunch with the head of an ad agency. I'll be back

after three, in time for the shoot. There's a whole stack
of films in the dark-room which need developing and
printing. Any problems—and there shouldn't be—just
ask Michael. Oh, and don't bother stopping for lunch
until you've done everything I've asked for.' His face
indicated that he thought this highly unlikely, and, with
nothing more than a brief nod which bore no courtesy
whatsoever, his long-legged frame swung across the
studio, and out.

CHAPTER THREE

YES, *sir*, thought Sam, as she watched Declan slam the door behind him, the pleasant smile fixed to her lips disguising her resentment at the way he had barked out his instructions. Drudge is my middle name.

But she set about the tasks he'd set her like a dervish, determined to redeem herself in his eyes.

Michael arrived a couple of minutes later, stuck his head round the studio door and gave Sam a wide grin. At least here's someone who's friendly, she thought, and gave him an answering smile.

He went straight away into his office at the front of the building, where he sat down at the computer and started tapping away, in between what seemed to Sam like the first of a hundred phone calls.

But although Sam worked hard, she scarcely seemed to notice how the time flew by; her thoughts were full of Declan, and the way she seemed to be reacting to him. It was as though all the feelings which she had put on ice as an eighteen-year-old after Bob's sickening betrayal had come to invade her years later, only the strength of those feelings seemed to be tangibly and shockingly stronger. But she had loved Bob, had been engaged to marry him—and yet she hadn't experienced anything like this kind of reaction with him.

Was it because over the years she had built up Declan in her mind as such a hero that she found it impossible to look on him as a mere mortal? Or could the reason be far more prosaic, that her feelings for Declan were nothing more than a very potent chemical reaction to a highly attractive man? Either way she had to get a grip on herself. It would be disastrous if Declan guessed her feelings, after all he'd said at the interview about emotional women.

Shortly before three, she was just finishing sweeping the studio floor when Michael stuck his head round the door, his eyes smiling from behind his John Lennon spectacles.

'Come and have some late lunch?' he suggested.

Well, she *had* completed the work Declan had set her, and it *had* been a long time since the piece of toast she'd eaten on the run first thing. She smiled. 'Thanks. That would be lovely.'

'Come through to the office. I still have to man the phone.'

Michael had made a pot of real coffee and a plate of cheese sandwiches. Sam took one and perched on the end of his desk before biting into it hungrily.

'Thanks. Declan gave me so much work that I didn't think I'd get any lunch.'

Michael laughed. 'He's just testing you.'

'*And* some!'

'Oh, his bark's much worse than his bite—don't take too much notice of Declan.'

Which was a little like telling her to ignore a cyclone in full swing. She suspected that Michael, as a man, would be immune to Declan with all his charm—all *she* needed to do was to try and build up the same kind of immunity. She looked at Michael curiously, and, catching her expression, he shrugged good-naturedly.

'Go on,' he said. 'Ask me.'

'Ask you what?'

'Why I'm working here.'

'It *is* rather an unusual job for a man to have,' she conceded.

'I love it,' said Michael simply. 'Speaking as a person who can't photograph a block of wood without messing it up, working for Declan allows me to indulge my love of photography vicariously. It's an exciting world he moves in, you know.'

'I can imagine. But——' she frowned and picked up another sandwich '—aren't you stuck in a—you know— rut?'

He shook his head. 'Declan pays me handsomely, and I am that rare breed—a man without ambition.'

Sam stared at him. 'Seriously?'

He nodded. 'Seriously. When I go home at night, I like to do just that. Switch off completely. If I were in some corporate hierarchy, I'd have to be back-stabbing with the rest of them. Late meetings, living on my nerves. No, thanks. I like to sit sedately on the sidelines.'

He pulled a demure face and Sam giggled. She felt safe with Michael—he didn't send her thoughts and senses into crazy turmoil. She tipped her head to one side, crossed her legs, and batted her eyelashes outrageously. 'Forgive me for saying this, Michael, but you'd make someone a great wife!'

He adopted an America drawl. 'Say—is that a proposal, honey?'

'I sincerely hope not,' came a deep, cold voice from the door, and Sam looked up to find Declan standing in the doorway, filling it with his muscular frame, his mouth a thin line of disapproval.

Sam felt like a child caught with her hand in the cookie jar, frozen in a ridiculous pose on Michael's desk like some flighty *femme fatale*. She uncrossed her legs and quickly stood up, her pulse again infuriating her by accelerating into its familiar dance as she stared up into that harshly handsome face and waited for the seemingly inevitable rebuke.

Michael, for one, seemed unconcerned. 'Hello, Declan,' he said. 'Will you ring Fran at home before four?'

Declan was still looking at Sam acidly. 'I thought I'd left you with enough work until I got back?'

She felt a warm glow of achievement. 'I've done it, actually,' she said sweetly.

He said nothing, but turned to Michael. 'I'd steer clear of Sam, if I were you—socially, I suspect she's a little wild for your taste, Mike.' He gave a nasty smile. 'Come through to the studio, will you, Sam?'

Still smarting from his last barb, Sam followed him, her eyes drawn unwillingly to the swing of the lean hips, and the line of the long, muscular legs covered by the clinging denim.

Once there, he cast his eye around at the immaculately tidy studio, and Sam met his gaze with triumphant challenge.

'Everything to your satisfaction—Declan?'

'Almost. I think we've established that your work is up to standard, so just let me give you a little word of warning about Michael.'

'*Michael*?' She found his steely look of disapproval inexplicable, and attempted to lighten the tension. 'He's a mass-murderer, right?'

There wasn't a flicker of answering humour. 'Let's get one thing straight, Sam, shall we? Michael is a very pleasant, easygoing man, but he isn't your type and, what's more, he has a loyal fiancée who adores him waiting for him at home.'

It would be almost laughable, thought Sam, except that he wasn't laughing. 'Just what are you suggest-ing——?'

'I'm *suggesting*,' he bit out, 'that you don't turn that big-brown-eyed look on him as though he's just per-sonally delivered the Holy Grail to you. Stick to the bread-roll-throwing types you normally hang around with. Oh——' and here his eyes became as stormy as the Atlantic Ocean '—do me one small favour, hmm? We know you're tiny, but you've proved you certainly aren't fragile, so do spare me that helpless-little-girl look when I speak to you. You're twenty-six, not eighteen.'

Pride made her meet his gaze without showing one iota of the hurt which clamped at her stomach at his needlessly cruel words. And, what was more, he was so unjustly wrong—about her, and about her supposed de-signs on Michael.

Determined that he shouldn't see how he had the power to wound her, she deliberately composed her face into an expression of mild concern. 'Shall I fetch you some Alka-Seltzer, Declan?' she asked in a honeyed voice.

He stared at her as though she'd had a brainstorm. 'What in hell's name are you on about?'

She raised her hands up in supplication. 'You seem out of sorts, that's all,' she replied, in a tone which was undisguised saccharin. 'I thought maybe that you might have indigestion—after your lunch.'

Their eyes met, and for a moment she thought that he was about to explode, when to her astonishment something which could almost have been humour curved one corner of his mouth into a tantalisingly crooked smile, but it was gone so quickly that she thought it was probably her own wish-fulfilment. Declan didn't smile; he snarled.

'Let's light the studio,' he snapped. 'The model arrives in ten minutes.'

And that battle appears to be over, thought Sam, as she set about assisting him.

They were shooting a costly diamond necklace for a leading diamond merchant's advertisement, and the model arrived along with a security guard who was carrying the jewellery, the art director of the advertising agency which was producing the advert, and an executive from the company which cut the gems. Sam made everyone coffee.

The model was called Nicki, a breathtakingly lovely creature of just seventeen, and Sam recognised that she had that indefinable quality about her which spelt stardom. She had the classic model combination of extreme height—most of it in her legs—waist-length curls, pouty lips and superb bone-structure. She made Sam feel like one of the seven dwarfs.

Determined to put Declan and her personal animosities aside, Sam set about making herself useful, rearranging light reflectors and positioning the wind machine which would make Nicki's glorious golden curls billow magnificently.

But Nicki was new to the business, and perhaps she was intimidated by Declan's reputation, because she was nervous as hell, Sam quickly realised, and her facial expressions became accordingly wooden. Sam sensed the assembled group holding their breath in anticipation, because they all knew that the success of the shoot depended on the model, and if she was unable to relax and Declan couldn't get the pictures he wanted then the whole shot would have to be rescheduled using a new model, both costly and time-consuming.

Declan looked up from his camera, a lock of dark hair falling over his forehead, and smiled. It was, thought Sam, a lethal and devastating combination. All that blatant masculinity coupled with blue eyes which could have melted ice. He smiled at Nicki.

'Is this your first job?'

His tone was nothing but kind and interested and perhaps the girl had been expecting censure, thought Sam, for she visibly relaxed in the sunshine of Declan's charm.

'My second, actually.'

He smiled again. 'You're doing well. This advert is going to appear in *Vogue*. Not bad for a second job.' He cupped his hands over an imaginary crystal ball and bent over it. 'I see great things ahead,' he intoned, in a trance-like voice, and Nicki giggled.

The chat continued, and Sam watched, fascinated, as he managed to wrest from her the rather astonishing fact that she was a keen gardener, and he even kept an intensely interested face when she proceeded to tell him all about the caterpillars which were attacking her camellia leaves! And he wasn't even flirting, Sam realised; he was far too clever and experienced to do that. In fact, Nicki herself was blooming because he was doing what probably no man had done since her youthful beauty had developed—he was treating her as an intelligent person, and not as a sex-object.

Seconds later he said to her, very casually, 'Right, are we ready to go?'

Nicki nodded, her eyes shining with hero-worship. You and me both, thought Sam regretfully. He doesn't even have to try. No wonder he's so arrogant.

He went back to the camera and began to focus in on the girl's face, while the dazzling diamonds sparked ice-fire at her neck. Sam knew without looking at any contact sheets that the pictures would be a masterpiece.

At six he said, 'It's a wrap.' And the jewels were packed away, the art director and the executive and Nicki all took their leave, all supremely satisfied with the day's work.

Sam cleared the studio, and when she'd finished she found Declan in the outer office, Michael long gone, leaning over the desk, lost in thought, silhouetted against the fading light.

As she stood silently behind him on the deep-pile carpet of the office, she thought that she had never seen someone standing quite so still. Was that a life-saving skill he'd learnt out in the East, while the battles raged all around him?

Sam stood for a moment studying him, a great rush of unwilling admiration washing over her as she imagined him remembering those days of trial and tribulation. Was he regretting them now, glad of the safety of his new world? Or did he miss the adrenalin coursing through his veins, the kind of feeling which no jewellery shoot— no matter how prestigious—could ever inspire?

And then her foolish imaginings disintegrated as her eyes were drawn to the focus of his attention. Lying to

one side of the desk was a large buff-coloured envelope—the hard-backed kind used to send photos. It
was marked 'confidential', and Michael had obviously
left it for Declan to open.

But it was the content of the envelope which filled her
mouth with a bitter taste. It was a large portrait-shot of
Gita.

Misty and provocative, she gazed lovingly at the
camera. And even from where she stood, Sam could see
some message scrawled in the corner, followed by a long
line of kisses. She drew in a breath and he turned round
instantly, before she had a chance to disguise the distaste
on her face. What was Gita doing sending him signed
photos with loving messages? Were her suspicions
founded in fact?

She saw his eyes harden like chips of sapphire. He
looked angry, as watchful as a cat. 'What is it?' he
snapped.

It was an abrupt, forbidding tone, and she wondered
if it was provoked by his guilt at coveting another man's
wife.

'What is it?' he repeated. 'Do you always make a habit
of sneaking up behind people like that?'

'I didn't "sneak up"—you just seemed very *lost in
thought*,' she retorted, and she knew that her voice con-
tained a quiet accusation, because his mouth twisted with
rage.

They stood staring at one another, Sam rooted to the
spot. There had been an intensity to the brief exchange
which seemed to spark off something in him. Something
very raw and basic. He was very angry—with her? Or
with Gita? But suddenly all his outward sophistication
fell away. She saw the man beneath, who had lain in

insect-ridden, sweaty jungles, getting shot at. His very maleness seemed to emanate from him in waves which were almost tangible, and she knew such terror and excitement that she took an unconscious step away from him. He saw the movement, and with lightning speed clamped his hand about her wrist and brought her up against him, so close that she could feel every tensed muscle like solid steel pressing against her soft curves.

The impact of his touch was explosive; she felt her body spring into instant clamouring response—as though he had somehow managed to place an electric charge deep inside her.

She stared up at him, both bewitched and petrified, and she saw his lips curve into a smile which was nothing whatsoever to do with happiness.

'Don't look so surprised,' he mocked softly. 'You must know by now what it does to a man when you gaze up at him with those big brown eyes. Like Bambi,' he mused, 'only not so innocent,' and he drew one thoughtful finger slowly down a cheek that she knew was drained of all blood. And that single contact, innocuous though it was, caused her insides to melt like butter on a hot day, and a shiver turned the skin beneath her clothes into icy goose-bumps. She was speechless and spellbound as she stared at him helplessly. She had never dreamed, *never*, that a man could make you feel like this. To feel so much, from so little...

He laughed then, almost ruthlessly, and let her go, turning to pick up the photo, sliding it back smoothly into its envelope, Gita's exquisite face mocking her as he did so.

Ignore it, she thought. Act flip—that's what he'd expect of you. Pretend it was nothing. *Nothing*. 'Will you be needing me for anything else tonight?' she asked coolly.

He gave her a quizzical look. 'In view of what just happened, I'd advise you to make your questions a little less ambiguous in future—a man could get quite the wrong idea.' He made for the door, then paused. 'As a matter of fact, I do—will you get those films developed tonight, before you go? Or is there a man waiting?'

If only he knew—and if he knew he'd never believe it in a million years. Let him think what he liked—anything rather than have him harbour fears that she had no life of her own, that he was going to become the main feature in it. She gave a little shrug. 'Kind of,' she prevaricated.

'Well, make sure he doesn't keep you out all night— we're out on location tomorrow, and it's an early start. We have to be in Sussex by eight, so I'll pick you up at six.'

Her brain must still be fuddled from that embrace, else why would she be stuttering out scarcely coherent replies? 'You mean—from my flat?'

His mouth twisted. 'Unless you'll be staying somewhere else?'

The implication was clear, and she shook her head, her eyes flashing with anger. 'I'll be at home.' Her voice was chilly.

He had his hand on the door-handle. 'Well—don't forget to lock up. Goodnight.'

'Goodnight.' Sam's stomach was churning as she took the film into the dark-room. What in heaven's name was happening to her? She snapped the light off and, by touch alone, wound the films on to their metal spirals and plunged them into developing fluid.

Her heart was racing like a piston. It was sexual attraction, nothing more, and she was going to have to hide it. Nothing had happened, and nothing would.

But her heart continued to race as she thought of tomorrow. Of a long drive to Sussex. Alone in the car with Declan.

CHAPTER FOUR

BY THE time Sam had finished at the studio, it was getting on for eight, and she had to dash like mad to get over to the youth club where she had been helping out on a weekly basis ever since she'd first arrived in London, almost eight years ago.

The club was in a dingy part of the city where the houses were small, grey and narrow, piled on top of one another with back-yards the size of pocket handkerchiefs. Her flat in Knightsbridge seemed almost palatial in comparison to the overcrowded tower blocks here, and had caused her a pang of guilt on more than one occasion.

Sam pushed open the door of the youth centre, to find that John had already arrived.

'Hi,' he smiled. 'How was your first day?'

She smiled back, pleased that he'd remembered. 'Don't ask.'

'That bad, huh?'

'I suppose there's a price to pay for being a genius,' she observed.

'The genius being Declan Hunt?'

'You've got it in one!' She began to fill the giant urn with water.

'And the price is?'

'That he's impossible!'

'You should work well together, then!'

'John!' Sam aimed a tea-cloth at his head which he caught perfectly. '*I* am not impossible!'

'Of course not, Sam!'

She watched him begin to fill jugs with orange and lemon squash.

Dear John. He'd been her closest friend since she'd arrived in London, still smarting with hurt and trying to get used to the fact that she wasn't going to be Bob's bride after all, that Charlotte had stepped in and taken over that particular role.

Angry, confused and alone, she had met John at a bus-stop near the Albert Hall in the driving rain. They had both been to the same Schumann concert and they had shared their views on the pianist over a cup of coffee which had extended into a supper of pasta, eating in John's book-filled but untidy flat.

He had been a friend when she'd most needed one; he had listened while she'd poured out her sense of bitter injustice at the treatment she'd received from the man she'd thought had loved her.

John was a social worker, impassioned and idealistic, and it was he who had persuaded Sam to lend a hand at the youth club he'd started. And what had begun as a method of filling her time and alleviating her pain had grown to become a pastime which gave her just as much as she put into it.

The evening, as ever, was sheer hard work, for which Sam was grateful because it enabled her to put all thoughts of Declan out of her head. But it wasn't all hard grind—there were moments of genuine delight and fun, and it was after eleven when she wearily let herself into her flat, picking up a small pile of mail and carrying it straight through to the sitting-room.

At least workwise her conscience was clear. She had not only developed the films, she had printed out sheets of contacts to send to the advertising agency tomorrow, so that they and the client could make their final choice of which photo would be used in the campaign.

She made herself coffee and sat down to read her post. Two bills, and a handwritten note from her next-door neighbours, asking if Sam would be able to feed their cat while they were away at the weekend. She would, of course, she could hardly say no, but caring for Macavity did rather conflict with her passion for ornithology. She had often seen him watching from a rooftop and licking his lips while the eager birds swooped down for the food she regularly provided for them. Well, as long as Macavity stayed with *her*, he could wear a bell on his collar, she decided.

There was also a letter from Flora.

Sam tore it open, her heart turning as she saw the carefully formed script, just imagining her seven-year-old niece laboriously writing it, her tongue protruding through her teeth as she did so, the way it always did when she was concentrating. The letter, as usual, spoke volumes. It read:

Dear Aunty Sammie, I hope you are well. I am very well but we can't have that puppy I told you about. Mummy says I will make it into a pet, and farms need working dogs, and she says that it will make a mess in the house. Did I tell you that we had it decorated? The sitting-room is called the drawing-room now.

Sam sighed. Over the years Charlotte's delusions of grandeur had obviously not diminished. The letter went on:

But we aren't allowed to do any drawing in it, and it is for the grown-ups only. Mummy says if I don't stop sucking my thumb then I will have to have a big metal brace on my teeth. I am trying, but it is hard. I miss you. Can I come to London and see you? Daddy says if it was a weekday he could bring me up on the train when he goes to work, and could take me home with him. Write soon. Love, Flora XXXX

There was, thought Sam, no reason why Flora shouldn't spend the day with her—she would love to have her. If it were on a weekday it would mean, of course, taking her into the studio with her—at least for part of the day. In which case she'd have to ask Declan if that would be OK. She remembered their earlier flare-up and decided that it might be prudent to wait a bit before cadging favours.

Her night was disturbed. Images of Flora became mixed up with images of an entirely different face, a harsh face from which deep blue eyes, as unremitting and as secretive as the sea, glittered at her like diamonds.

Restlessly, burning up with a strange kind of heat, she tossed and turned, the duvet sliding from her on more than one occasion, until in the end she kicked it off completely, the half-open window sending welcoming drifts of cool breeze over her body, clothed in nothing but a thin cotton nightdress...

She awoke to a noise which relentlessly and noisily jabbed at her consciousness and fuzzily she turned to her bedside locker, discovering to her horror that it was now ten past six, and that she had slept right through the alarm.

The doorbell rang loudly again but this time it did not stop, and, cursing underneath her breath, Sam pulled on her oversized towelling dressing-gown, and hurried barefooted across the carpet.

She threw open the front door to find Declan standing there, dressed in black jeans and a black cashmere sweater over which he wore a faded brown leather flying jacket, his hand leaning on the doorbell, a look of irritation crossing his face as he took in her state of undress.

'You've got five minutes,' he snapped. 'After that, you come as you are. So if you don't fancy spending the day in your boyfriend's dressing-gown, I'd advise you to get a move on.'

As she was still muzzy from her rudely awakened sleep, it took a moment for it to register what he'd said as she stumbled back into her bedroom. Her *boyfriend's* dressing-gown? Very funny. And what if it had been? Even if she had been sleeping with her boyfriend, if she *had* a boyfriend—which she didn't—well, that was perfectly normal in this day and age. There was certainly no reason for Declan to imply that she was some sort of fallen woman.

She pulled off the offending garment, and followed it with the cotton nightdress. He was very fond of leaping to conclusions, she decided, as she splashed icy-cold water all over her still-rosy cheeks. She wore a man's robe because, in the absence of a suitable male, she liked it to snuggle into on cold winter evenings. She realised that for some reason there was just no pleasing Declan— if she'd appeared wearing some flimsy lacy négligé, he would doubtless still have made some acerbic comment.

She dressed quickly in old blue jeans and a thick Arran sweater and went back into the sitting-room, where he stood with his back to the fireplace, taking in every inch of the luxuriously appointed flat with all its expensive, if soulless fittings. His expression told her that it was exactly the kind of place he had visualised her living in. Poor little rich girl, his moody eyes seemed to say as they flicked over her briefly.

'You'll need a coat,' he said abruptly. 'It's raining.'

'Right.' Her green waxed jacket hung on the coat-stand, and she was just wriggling into it when there was a hopeful chirrup from outside and Sam hurried over to the windowsill, picked up a bag of nuts and raised the sash window.

'What the *hell*?' he demanded.

'It'll only take a second,' she said, as she tipped a handful of peanuts into a wire container which hung from the window, noting that a greenfinch was hovering hopefully.

His face was a picture. 'Let's go,' he snarled.

She didn't argue, just hurried after him.

He had a long, low black sportscar and she climbed in next to him and buckled herself in. He immediately pushed a cassette into the stereo—of some obscure violin concerto which she didn't recognise, and which she took as a not very subtle hint he didn't intend chatting to her. She leaned back in her seat and tried to concentrate on the landscape which was flashing by them, but she found it very difficult not to send little side-glances at those magnificently long and muscular legs as his feet moved over the pedals of the car.

He drove with practised ease, fast and decisively—he would, she realised, do everything with that same confident skill. That was how he would make love, too, a small voice uttered with wicked temptation, and she felt herself tremble a little. This was *madness*—sheer, bloody madness. You're becoming obsessed, fixated on a man who is light-years away from you, behaving as if you'd never been out with a man before. And this is work, don't forget. Your career is on the line here, so jolly well snap out of it. Pushing all her conflicting thoughts to the back of her mind, she spoke hurriedly.

'What's the job today?' She should have got the details from the diary, she realised.

Surprisingly, he didn't chastise her; perhaps he remembered that she'd worked late. 'More jewellery. Only this time it's paste. Up-market costume gems. The agency wants the models picnicking in evening-gowns and the place we're going to is perfect.'

'And who are the models?'

He glanced at her briefly. 'Jade Westbrook and Chrissie Bennett. Do you know them?'

'Not really. I've worked with Chrissie once,' she said carefully. And once too often. The model was stunning, but with a reputation for bitchiness which was well-earned.

'She's good—the camera loves her. Though I know she does have a reputation for being—temperamental.'

And that, thought Sam, could be classified as the understatement of the year. Only a man would class Chrissie as 'temperamental'! She had heard a much richer selection of adjectives used—though it wouldn't do to repeat them to him. 'So I believe,' she said neutrally, and saw him give a small smile.

The drive took a little over an hour, and as they drove the rain stopped, although the clouds remained ominous.

They had chosen a poppy field for the shoot, a heavenly blaze of scarlet, and Sam couldn't stop herself from giving a small squeal as the black car rounded the bend and drew towards the brilliant red haze.

He slowed down immediately. 'What is it?'

She pointed ahead. 'Oh, it's *perfect*! Magnificent. Even in the early morning light—it looks just like a Monet painting with those great big splashes of red!'

A brief light of amusement flared in his eyes. 'Such touching enthusiasm,' he responded drily, as he parked in front of the iron-barred gate. 'It's funny, I didn't have you down as an art lover.'

He wasn't going to get away with *that*. 'But photography's art, surely?'

He laughed. '*Touché*. You know what I mean. Your—er—flat.'

Sam turned to open her door. Yes, she knew what he meant. There was little to commend the safe, deadly dull limited editions which hung in her flat, chosen primarily for the way they matched the furniture. Well, she wasn't going to defend herself by telling him that the décor hadn't been of her choosing—let him think what he liked.

She helped him carry the two cameras into the middle of the field, and minutes later the others arrived. The crew was larger than usual—there was a make-up artist and a hairdresser in tow. To Sam's surprise, the make-up artist was the same stunning redhead she'd seen Declan lunching with in the restaurant that day.

Close up, she was even more attractive—she could have been a model herself, thought Sam resignedly, as she watched Declan's face light up. As jobs went, working with beautiful women day in and day out didn't exactly do a lot for the ego.

'Fran,' he said warmly, and kissed her on both cheeks. 'How are you?'

'I'm fine, Declan, just fine. Settling nicely into my new flat and——'

'When you've *quite* finished exchanging your life histories—I need some lacquer on my hair, Fran,' interrupted Chrissie rudely. 'Don't I get a kiss, then, Declan?' she pouted, her full lips gleaming with provocation.

'Love to,' he replied smoothly. 'But the make-up artist would kill me!'

Which got him neatly out of that one, thought Sam. Not a man to be manipulated, then. As she handed him his camera, she wondered, slightly hysterically, whether on every shoot the various female members of the crew spent the entire time fighting for the favours of Declan Hunt!

It was a troublesome shoot as shoots went. The light kept fading, and rain threatened all morning until noon when, with a great hissing sound, the clouds finally burst.

'Right—let's break for lunch!' shouted Declan. 'Sam—get that umbrella over here quickly.'

They found a nearby restaurant where Declan seated himself next to Fran and was chatting animatedly to her, but Sam could see from the light of battle which gleamed in Chrissie's beautiful blue eyes that hostilities were about to be resumed.

'So what's it like being back in England, Declan?' she began. 'And why did you leave the States? Not homesick, surely?'

He shrugged. 'Not a bit. I liked the States very much— but I never intended to live there forever.'

'No?' Chrissie ran her tongue over her bottom lip, in as obvious a provocative gesture as Sam had ever seen.

'And now you're back, of course, everyone will be wanting to know whether you'll be taking any pictures of Gita?'

Sam could feel the tension in the air immediately; it surrounded Declan like an aura. She watched Fran's hand still in the process of stirring her coffee, and an uncomfortable look cross her face.

Declan's face was a hard slash of rigid angles, the eyes mere slits. 'Gita doesn't model any more,' he said abruptly.

'No, I know. But I'm sure she'd be more than willing to make an exception—for *you*, Declan.'

As an allusion it was crystal-clear, thought Sam, a sick feeling at the pit of her stomach as she scanned her menu. She tried to tell herself that her feelings of anger were inspired by loyalty to her ex-boss, but she realised in that instant that they were rooted in a far more fundamental cause than that. You're *jealous*, she thought in surprise. Jealous of Gita.

'Sam...?' Narrowed blue eyes were staring at her quizzically, as she discovered that the waitress was waiting to take her order. 'What are you eating?'

'I'll have the chicken.' She watched as Declan, apparently unperturbed, ordered drinks. It's none of my business what he does in his life, she thought angrily. I'm his employee, not his moral guardian.

But her appetite had deserted her and the chicken in its creamy mushroom sauce made her feel very slightly sick, so that she picked at the food like a convalescent before pushing her plate away.

'Watching our weight, are we?' enquired Chrissie sweetly. 'I'm not surprised. Being so small, every extra *ounce* must show, although, I must say, that sweater you're wearing hides a multitude of sins.'

There was a silence around the table as Sam flushed scarlet at the insult. The impact of growing up with a beautiful blonde mother and sister when you were small and fairly insignificant had inevitably left its mark. People hadn't *meant* to be unkind, but often, unthinkingly, they had been. Sam had grown used to the tactless remarks directed at her mother by well-meaning friends— 'You mean *this* is Sam? Goodness me, Jayne—who *can* she take after? There's not a bit of you in her!'

But Chrissie's remark wasn't merely tactless, it was downright bitchy. Hours later Sam would probably be able to compose a witty retort, but for now she was struck dumb and as the silence grew it made the atmosphere even worse.

A pair of piercing blue eyes were turned in her direction, a slight puzzlement in them, as if he was expecting her to snap back at Chrissie, not sit mute and blushing like a fool. And then her plate was pushed firmly towards her, and a deep voice said, 'Sam doesn't need to diet. She may be small, but she's perfectly formed.' Then more quietly, 'Eat your lunch, Sam. You didn't have any breakfast.'

A buzz of chatter broke out as he defused the situation, and Sam picked up her knife and fork, her feelings confused. She was grateful to him, yes, for being so gallant. And flattered by the compliment, even if he didn't mean it. But angry, too. He had Fran, and probably Gita, too, and he'd never look at her in a million years, and yet he was succeeding in making her fall for him.

Just sexual attraction, she had thought, but no, it was more than that. She wanted to find out what made him tick, to find out why he was wasting his talent by working taking photos of women like Chrissie wearing over-priced baubles.

Lunch over, and the rain gone, they resumed work and Sam was glad when Declan finally got the photos he wanted and everyone left, leaving just the two of them to pack up their equipment.

He looked at her as she heaved his Hasselblad camera into the boot.

'Chrissie was foul to you. I'm sorry.'

She was taken aback. 'Why should you be sorry? It isn't anything to do with you.'

'She was angry with me, and she took it out on you.'

'Why was she angry with you?'

He shrugged. 'It isn't important.'

But he didn't need to tell her why. She understood perfectly. Chrissie had been behaving coquettishly to-wards Declan all morning, and he had not bitten. For a beautiful woman such rejection must be hard. And somehow Sam didn't think that there had been a past relationship, either—he didn't strike her as the kind of man who would cast off his ex-girlfriends discourteously.

He glanced at a slim watch which glittered discreetly on his tanned wrist. 'We'd better get going. The rush-hour starts earlier and earlier these days.'

Which turned out to be famous last words, because while driving along the notorious M25 they slowed to a complete halt.

'Damn!' swore Declan.

Sam creased her eyes as she peered up ahead. 'What is it?'

'I can see what looks like a number of cans strewn all over the road. A lorry appears to have shed its load.' He sounded impatient.

'So what do we do?'

He turned the engine off with a quick flick. 'What we do is wait.'

'Oh.' The car suddenly seemed very small. There were no cameras to distract them, no light meters to play with. Nothing to do but for her to sit there growing uncomfortably aware of how much he affected her. She wished he'd put the radio on, but she supposed that would be unwise with the engine switched off.

'Were you pleased with the shoot?' she babbled.

'Mmm?' He seemed distracted, tapping his long fingers on the steering-wheel in a primitive beat. 'So tell me,' he said suddenly. 'Why do I keep getting muddled messages about you?'

'What—are you talking about?' she stuttered. Oh, God—was her body language so blatant that he knew that she was squirming inwardly with a need to have him pull her into his arms?

'Which is the real Sam Gilbert, I wonder?' he asked softly. 'She mixes with drunken hooray Henrys and lives in an expensive flat in Knightsbridge which her wages wouldn't even pay one-tenth of. But that Sam Gilbert doesn't marry at all well with the one who blushes the way you did this morning, leaves nuts out for the birds, and takes pictures of small children with an obvious love of them shining through, which is fairly unusual for a woman who isn't a mother.'

'You mean that I don't fit into your stereotyping of me?' she retorted. 'You made a snap judgement of me which you never considered might be wrong.'

'Ah, but first impressions count, you can't deny that. And I'm interested to know how you can afford to live in one of the best parts of London.'

She knew that he was only making conversation to pass the time, but she found his tone presumptuous. 'Can't you guess? My sugar daddy pays.'

He actually laughed, and for some reason this infuriated her even more.

'You think that's so funny?' she demanded.

'I think it's highly unlikely, that's all. Sugar daddies don't usually choose women whose——' he stared down at her, and the blue eyes suddenly darkened '—faces are all pink and scrubbed, hair all windswept, wearing no mascara.'

His voice had deepened too, and for one moment of insanity she thought that he was about to bend that dark head, leaving those harsh, beautiful features hovering just inches away before claiming her in a kiss that she instinctively knew would send her hurtling into another stratosphere.

But he didn't kiss her; her imagination was playing games with her—and, if she analysed what he'd just said, he was implying that sugar daddies liked their women glamorous . . . and that was one thing no one could ever accuse her of being.

'You're right, of course. The flat belongs to a friend of my mother.'

A dark eyebrow was raised in question as he registered the tone of her voice. 'Oh?'

She sighed, reluctant to tell him, but anything was better than having to endure a silence which meant that her thoughts could spin out of control... 'It used to belong to my mother. You know she was Jayne Carrol—the model?'

He nodded. 'I believe Charlotte mentioned it.'

'She bought the flat when she first came to London, years ago—before she met my father. Then, after they got married and they moved to the country, she wanted to keep it on, even though she only used it infrequently.'

'An expensive bolt-hole?' he suggested.

'Well, yes. Too expensive, eventually. It always caused friction between my parents, but to my mother it was always more than just a flat—it was a symbol of all she achieved in her career. A symbol of her youth, if you like.' A gilded youth which all her mother's time and money were now spent trying to emulate. 'Five years ago she sold it to a friend of hers who married some American tycoon. For tax purposes, so I understand. And the deal was that our family could always use it as much as we wanted—because they don't use it themselves much—a couple of trips a year or so. But next year their daughter will be studying over here—so she'll move in, too. I'm there mainly as a deterrent to squatters. They only charge me a peppercorn rent—which is fortunate, as I couldn't manage on what you pay me.' She lifted her chin in a gesture of defiant pride. It suddenly seemed terribly important that she dispel his image of her as some spoilt little rich girl. 'I don't get an allowance, you know—I manage on what I earn. I make most of my own clothes!'

'Do you?' he said thoughtfully.

She felt that she had given away too much of herself, and this put her at a disadvantage. Suddenly, she wanted to know something about *him*, something to redress the balance.

'And what about your parents, Declan?'

'They're dead.' Flatly unequivocal, his tone warned her off. And while it seemed that she had given him *carte blanche* to interrogate her, his profile had taken on a harshly indifferent look which forbade further questioning.

'The traffic's moving.' There was unmistakable relief in his voice, which he didn't bother trying to disguise.

He was probably regretting the interest he'd shown, afraid it might give his gauche little assistant the wrong idea.

But when they drew up outside her flat, his next words astonished her.

'The last Saturday of the month. On the twenty-ninth. Are you free—in the evening?'

Over three weeks away. Her eyes lit up. 'I—think so,' she stumbled, feeling like Cinderella.

'There's an awards ceremony at the Beaumont hotel— I have to go—and you might as well come along with me.'

'I——' She felt excited, breathless with it, and not slick enough to disguise it. 'That sounds wonderful.'

His mouth curved a little as he shot her a quick glance. 'Don't get too excited about it. It's only work.'

A bludgeon blow to her foolish dreams. She forced a question. 'And what about Fran?'

'Fran?'

'Fran—your friend. The make-up artist. Doesn't she want to go?'

He looked as though he resented the intrusive question. 'Fran will be out of the country that night, otherwise yes, I'd probably take her.'

That told her. She struggled to push the door open. 'Thanks.'

'Don't mention it. I'll see you tomorrow. Goodnight.'

'Goodnight.' She climbed out of the car and made her way up the steps to her front door, catching a last glimpse of that tanned, harshly handsome profile, with the dark curls brushing the sheepskin collar of his flying jacket. She could have stared at him all night, but she forced herself to turn her back and take out her keys, not reacting as he roared away in the powerful car.

CHAPTER FIVE

DURING the next few weeks, Declan didn't mention the awards ceremony—instead he showed her just how hard he expected her to work. She would learn under his tutelage, yes, but at what a price—by the end of each day she was absolutely *exhausted*.

Declan was so different from Robin—his undoubted genius behind the lens made him demanding, autocratic, always instinctively right where his work was concerned. He was a perfectionist who broke every rule in the book, a man, she quickly realised, who could never be pigeonholed.

She had always respected his work; she soon grew to respect the man and, infuriatingly, much as she tried to resist, she continued to react to his potent masculinity like a bee to honey.

One evening, when they had worked companionably until almost ten o'clock, she plucked up courage to ask him about Flora.

'Er—Declan?'

He looked up briefly. 'What?'

'I had a letter from my niece, Flora—Charlotte's daughter.'

'Very enlightening, Sam,' he said sarcastically. 'But I don't see what that has to do with me.'

She had been expecting a response like that—his bark *was* worse than his bite. She ignored it and continued unperturbed. 'She's keen to come up to London—her

father can bring her on a weekday—that would—er—
mean——'

'Is this your roundabout way of asking for time off?'

She gave him a serene smile. 'Well, I *have* put in a lot
of overtime. What would be great, actually, would be if
I brought her in the morning—she says she wants to be
a photographer, you see.'

'I'm not having children running riot in the studio,'
he said flatly. 'Apart from anything else, it's dangerous.'

'She's very sensible,' insisted Sam.

'She'd better be,' he answered darkly. 'And you're re-
sponsible for her while she's here—understand?'

Victory! 'Yes, Declan,' she replied happily. 'Then if
I could have the afternoon off—I could take her to see
a matinee . . .'

He gave her a warning look to which she responded
with a silent glance at her watch, which showed that it
was now almost ten-thirty, and they'd been in the studio
since seven.

'Oh, very well,' he said grudgingly. 'Now can you cut
the chat and develop this film for me?'

A week later Flora, in workaday denim dungarees, her
ginger hair in practical plaits, was hugely impressed with
the cavernous studio, and *hugely* impressed with Declan.

'I hear you're going to be a photographer when you're
older?' he said gravely.

Flora nodded eagerly. 'Oh, yes, Mr Hunt—'

'Declan.'

'Declan.' She gave him a gap-toothed grin. 'Just like
you!'

'Not like Sam?' he questioned.

She shook her head. 'Oh, no. Aunty Sammie says that *you're* the best photographer in the whole world——'

'Flora!' shrieked Sam, scarlet with mortification, meeting his amused stare defiantly.

'Why, thank you, Sam,' he murmured. 'Lavish praise indeed.'

Her face told him that if her seven-year-old niece hadn't been there she would have responded very tartly indeed!

He let Flora stay in the studio for the shoot, and afterwards insisted that she take a whole roll of film herself of a very embarrassed Sam. Then, while Sam reloaded all the various cameras, Declan gave step-by-step instructions to Flora.

Michael came in while they were doing this, three heads bent intently over the camera, Declan and Flora on either side of Sam, who was trying very hard to stop her fingers from shaking.

'Such harmony!' teased Michael.

Sam went pink and Declan growled something softly underneath his breath and disappeared for the rest of the morning.

Sam had promised Flora a hamburger lunch.

'Is Declan coming?'

'Coming where?' he said as he came out of the office carrying a cup of coffee.

'To Hamburger Heaven. Aunty Sammie's taking me there.'

'Declan's busy, darling,' said Sam quickly.

He glanced down at her, and then at Flora's disappointed face.

'Do they do milkshakes?' he asked.

Flora turned a freckled face upwards. '*Do* they, Aunty Sammie?' she asked anxiously.

'Every flavour under the sun,' answered Sam steadily.

'Well, I'll come on one condition.' He smiled down at Flora. 'That I can have double chocolate!'

Hamburger Heaven was an appropriately named restaurant, Sam decided—because having lunch with Declan and Flora really *was* heaven. Which seemed to demonstrate further her own lack of sophistication—for wasn't it slightly pathetic that the most memorable meal in the life of a twenty-six-year-old should have been sitting watching a dark, broad-shouldered man sitting dunking his fries in ketchup?

He revealed a side of himself that Sam wouldn't have dreamed existed. With Flora he was gentle, caring, funny. She watched him clowning around, twisting the free balloon into a rabbit shape, with Flora responding with giggling gratitude, while their waitress, who'd clearly recognised him, actually wrote her phone number on top of the bill!

But next morning, when Sam showed up for work, his manner was as caustic as ever, as though he was trying to tell her that cosy lunches with small girls and small women who thought he was the cat's whiskers with a camera were out!

His cool behaviour persisted all week, until the evening before the awards when he said in a faintly bored tone, 'I'll be round at eight,' which sent her blood-pressure soaring with temper—he could have *pretended* a little interest, surely?

By six-thirty on Saturday, Sam was in a high old state of nerves. It didn't seem to matter that this was merely a duty evening, that Declan obviously regarded it as a

chore to be got through, because she found herself
wanting to effect a complete transformation to knock
his socks off when he arrived. Which was why her ex-
pertly sewn dresses in hues of saffron, vermilion and
jade all lay in bright disregarded heaps on the bed
awaiting her final decision.

She looked in the mirror and sighed.

She had just decided that perhaps the cerise silk might
be most suitable—although the colour *was* a little dazzling—when the telephone rang.

An hour later, still in her jeans, she opened the door
to Declan. He made an unbelievably striking vision in
the formal suit. The austere lines of his dinner-jacket
illustrated the width of his shoulders, while the unbut-
toned jacket gave an occasional tantalising glimpse of
the firm, taut torso which lay beneath the fine silk of
his shirt. The black tapered trousers, with the satin trim
down the outer leg, made his legs look even longer than
they did in the faded denim he normally wore. He had
even managed to tame the unruly dark curls into something resembling a fairly sedate haircut, but already one
demon lock had started to fall over the tanned forehead.

He took one look at her and tensed his brows together
in a look of anger which immediately became one of
surprise.

'You've been crying,' he stated. 'What's happened—
nail-polish chipped?'

She wasn't in any sort of mood for his sarcasm tonight. 'I'm sorry, but I can't come to the awards with
you, Declan.'

He completely ignored her and walked straight into
the flat. 'On the contrary. You can, and you will. I
thought you didn't cry.'

'I don't—ususally.'

'So why the tears?'

She shook her head. 'Something that happened earlier today.'

'Mmm?' His face was implacable.

She shook her head, the hair she had intended to crimp still damp from the shower and flying in limp tendrils around her face. 'Won't you just go on without me?'

'I'm not going anywhere until you tell me what's made you cry.'

She was never normally this lachrymose, and she found she was having difficulty keeping her voice steady. 'There's a youth club,' she stumbled, 'that I sometimes help out at.'

'Sometimes?'

'Once, sometimes twice a week. It was started by John; he's a social worker—friend of mine.'

He looked at her steadily, but said nothing.

'It's a great scheme.' Impossible to keep the pride out of her voice. 'Because it's not just for able-bodied kids. We take kids with a physical disablement too. When we started mixing the two groups, everyone benefited. The tough kids got softer and protective—and somehow the kids who'd maybe had problems accepting their disability. . . they became more positive.'

'And that makes you cry?'

'No, damn you!' Her voice trembled, but the words were out before she could stop them, not angry with him, but lashing out at him blindly. 'I'll tell you what makes me cry. We were due to have a disco there next week. The hall was broken into last night—the stereo was stolen, the place vandalised. Everything wrecked.

Everything. We survive on voluntary contributions as it is—but we think that this might be it for the club.'

'Get dressed,' he said curtly.

It was as though he hadn't heard a word she'd been saying. She stared at him in disbelief. 'I can't go, knowing——'

'Get dressed. We'll visit your club on the way.'

'But we'll be late.'

'A few minutes. It doesn't matter.'

She shook her head. 'I can't go there in all my party finery—it'll be like rubbing their noses in it.'

'So you'll patronise them by dressing down?'

'Don't you dare speak to me like that.' Her voice was quiet with anger.

'Then get changed. They aren't fools, Sam. You do your best for them, but you aren't like them. You live in a bloody great flat in Knightsbridge for a start. Stop trying to be something you're not—they won't mind.'

He almost sounded gentle, and that knocked out the last bit of fight in her. Feeling subdued, she turned and went back into the bedroom, and returned minutes later wearing a grey-black silk dress, her hair brushed and beginning to gleam as it dried.

'Come on,' he said, and put his hand lightly on the small of her back to usher her out.

She tried not to sink back against him, she fought to try to stay immune, but failed. It isn't fair, she thought desperately, as the car roared off towards the Elephant and Castle—either he knows the effect he has on women and doesn't care, or he likes playing games, making them fall for him, as I'm in danger of doing. But he doesn't *have* to play games, corrected a small voice in her head. Women fall for him without him having to lift a finger.

So perhaps he really *wasn't* aware of the way her senses sang with delirious joy whenever he so much as touched her, even when she was feeling as miserable as sin about the theft. For the rest of the journey he quizzed her gently about the club, and she directed him to the run-down part of the city which housed it.

They walked into the club to find total chaos. Sam's heart plummeted.

'Oh, it's awful,' she lamented. 'How *can* they? How *can* people do such a thing?'

He ran his eyes over the room swiftly and assessingly. 'It's not as bad as it looks,' he contradicted. 'Overturned chairs can soon be righted, that window mended—the obscenities painted out.'

A small, wiry young man in his late twenties with curly blond hair came towards them.

Sam stepped forward. 'John—this is Declan Hunt, my boss. Declan, this is John Miles—the social worker I told you about.'

Both men looked at each other squarely, before Declan held out his hand. 'Pleased to meet you, John. Sam's told me a little about the place. I'm sorry about the break-in, but I might be able to help.' He smiled. 'The sound system bit's simple enough—I've an old stereo which I never use now. You can have that with pleasure.'

John thanked him, a little stiffly, thought Sam, but then perhaps he thought that Declan looked rather overpowering standing in the scruffy club in all his dark, dinner-suited glory—she knew that *she* certainly thought so.

There was the hint of a smile on Declan's face as he acknowledged the thanks. 'Tomorrow's Sunday—does the group meet then?'

John nodded. 'In the morning. Between ten and twelve.'

'I'd like to come round with my camera, take a few shots—if that's OK?'

'What for?' asked Sam.

'Because pictures have an impact that words don't. Let's get people indignant about what's happened. I have a mate on one of the nationals—let me see what I can do.'

'That's very kind of you,' said John, visibly relaxing, his smile now threatening to split his face in two.

In the car on the way to the awards, Sam turned towards Declan. 'You've been terribly generous,' she said. 'I don't think I've ever seen John look quite so delighted.'

He shot her a swift glance. 'Have you known him for very long?'

'As long as I've been in London. He's been a good friend.'

'I see,' he said, then lapsed into silence.

And that, she thought, was that.

The interior of the Beaumont hotel was awash with glamour. Satin and taffeta abounded, but the most striking substance on display was bare flesh. In her simple grey-black dress, Sam suddenly felt like a tadpole trapped in an aquarium of vividly exotic fish.

It was a new experience for her to be out with such an outrageously good-looking man. She had been aware of that since the moment they'd arrived; his height and his striking looks had made him an instant focus of attention. And yet he seemed strangely ill at ease, the dark blue eyes narrowed, looking for a moment like a tiger who had been offered a saucer of milk in a suburban sitting-room. She wondered what had caused it, and then she caught the direction of his glance, and stilled.

Gita. Holding court.

As always, Sam was struck by the sheer perfection of her body and face. Her jet-black hair was pulled back off her brow and caught up in a gold comb from which it fell in one dark shimmering curtain to her waist. She was impossibly tall and slender—she towered over Robin—and tonight she wore a gown of gold tissue clinging to every pore, so that she resembled some age-old goddess men would always pay homage to.

The huge glittering dark eyes were drawn to Declan's face as if compelled to do so. They swept over him in unashamed appraisal, and then she smiled, a secret, pussycat smile.

Conversation had hushed, and Sam felt like a gladiatorial spectator.

'Come,' said Declan, and to her horror he propelled her towards Gita's table.

Surely he wasn't going to have the gall to go up and speak to her, with Robin looking daggers?

It seemed that he was.

'Hello, Robin; Gita,' he said smoothly. 'How well you both look.'

'And you, too,' purred Gita.

Even her voice was exquisite, thought Sam. She had been educated at one of the best schools in England, and her softly modulated, almost bell-like tones contrasted dramatically with her exotic beauty.

Gita's eyes flicked once over Sam, then turned back to her ex-lover. 'You've been avoiding us since you got back from the States, Declan,' she remonstrated.

'Pressure of work,' smiled Declan, holding up his hands in the comical manner of a head-waiter who was telling a group of diners he had no more tables.

'Sit down.'

It was an imperious command, but he fielded it neatly. 'Perhaps later. I've promised Sam that I'd listen to her opinion of the prizewinners.'

The air fizzled with tension and Sam felt sick. He can't bear to sit with her and her husband, she thought bitterly. If he didn't care it wouldn't matter. He cares. He's still in love with her.

'Hello, Sam.' Eyes that glittered like black diamonds were turned in her direction. 'Are you enjoying your new job?'

'Very much,' replied Sam.

'Well,' Gita smiled, 'I hope that Declan's behaving himself. I used to be his assistant—oh, *years* ago—and there were definitely perks to the job, as I can vouch. Very good perks they were, too.'

Sam felt like throwing up. How *could* she? How could she humiliate Robin like that by openly boasting of Declan's sexual prowess? She stared up at Declan helplessly, but his features remained as implacable as if they had been hewn from some cold, dark rock.

'Have a pleasant evening,' he said. 'Now if you'll excuse us?'

Sam followed him across the room—where the crowd seemed to open up for him as if he were Moses parting the waves—the sick feeling in her stomach not subsiding.

It was blatant—*blatant*. Gita had smouldered with passion for Declan. Had she realised her mistake, that a title meant nothing when you didn't have the man you loved? And if she had decided that she would throw it all away to regain Declan, then what man in his right mind could resist a woman like that?

Sam knew that there were eyes on them as they followed the arrows towards one of the ante-rooms, aware of the second glances they were attracting. For Sam, it was a new and not very welcome experience. She knew that she made the best of her small, delicate features and disguised the slight over-lushness of her breasts as best she could, but she was not the kind of woman who men looked at twice—or women, for that matter—and she was certainly being looked over twice tonight. And she could read in their eyes the silent question—what the hell is *he* doing with someone like *her*?

Had she been invited here tonight as a kind of social cover-up, with Declan sending some kind of subtle message to Gita: that she was his colleague, and so obviously not the kind of woman he would be attracted to that Gita could feel quite safe?

She was glad when they reached the photos, determined to escape the confusion of her thoughts and to lose herself in the private world which every good photograph created.

'And marks out of ten?'

The deep voice brought her back to reality with a heart-wrenching jolt. He was pointing to a beautifully lit black and white portrait of a mother and child she'd been studying. She liked looking at pictures of children almost more than anything—before they learnt to disguise their emotions for the camera—but she didn't like this one.

'I don't like it very much,' she told him.

'Oh?' It obviously wasn't what he was expecting to hear, because she saw the dark eyebrows knit together in surprise. 'One of France's finest photographers?'

'That doesn't necessarily mean it's a great picture. I think it's contrived.'

'Contrived?' He studied it again. 'Why?'

She shrugged. 'It's too—*perfect*. You can tell that the model isn't the baby's real mother.'

'Can you now?' he asked softly.

The frustration she'd been feeling since the encounter with Gita made her more vociferous than normal. 'Of course you can!' she declared. 'The model's so beautiful, so elegant, so groomed. Most mothers with a baby of that age have great rings underneath their eyes because they haven't been sleeping. The signs of ''baby-shock'', as they call it, are all over them.'

'You being an expert on babies, I suppose?'

She jerked her thumb at the picture. 'Probably much more than he is!' she declared rashly.

She saw him smile. 'So what you're saying is that for art to be good it's got to show your subject as it really is, warts and all?'

She forced herself to calm down. We're having a serious discussion, she thought. *That's* why you came to work for him. It isn't fair to be angry with him just because you wish he were making love to you. 'I suppose that *is* what I'm saying,' she said slowly. 'This is good in its way—as a demonstration of light and shade, it's superb. But real life it isn't.'

'Keep your voice down.' He sounded amused. 'Here comes Jean-Claude himself.'

Jean-Claude Martin had ignored the instructions for 'dress suit' on the invitation, to appear looking like every cartoonist's idea of a typically handsome Frenchman. He wore a Breton shirt over white jeans, with a red scarf knotted at his throat, and with his olive complexion and flashing dark eyes Sam half expected him to wheel in his bicycle and throw a string of onions over his shoulder!

'*Alors, Hunter*!' he exclaimed. '*Ça va?*'

'*Très bien, merci,*' Declan replied instantly and with impeccable accent.

Show-off, thought Sam, then went slightly pink as she caught him studying her, a glint in his eyes as if he'd read her thoughts.

'Allow me to introduce you to my new assistant—Sam Gilbert.'

'Sam? But it is a man's name, and she is a beautiful woman!' he protested.

'Jean-Claude invented the word "compliment",' said Declan drily.

'The secret of my success!' White teeth flashed in the handsome olive face. 'You like my picture?'

Sam's eyes met Declan's. She saw the light of challenge there and returned it, her resentment of Gita and her frustrated passion making her want to do combat with him, to fence with him verbally.

Liar.

What she really wanted was for him to kiss her. Kiss her and never stop.

'Sam's just been admiring your picture, haven't you, Sam?' came a deep, mocking voice.

She stared back at him. *You wouldn't dare*, her eyes said.

Jean-Claude seemed oblivious to the silent little tussle. 'Of Giscard? Yes, indeed—he is a beautiful boy, *mon fils.*'

'Your *son*?' asked Sam in bewilderment. 'And the model?'

'Marie-Claire—my wife,' he said proudly.

They chatted for a few seconds more, and then Jean-Claude left them.

Sam turned on him. 'You *knew* didn't you? That she was his wife—and the child's mother. And you let me rant on, making a fool of myself——'

'Not a fool of yourself.' He shook his head. 'I liked it. You have a certain—passion. An enthusiasm. When you analyse photos; when you look at fields of poppies.'

He didn't realise that it was like bread to a starving man to hear him give her even the smallest compliment. And it meant nothing. She strove to wound. 'You used to have it, too, didn't you, Declan? You had passion, too. You used to take photos which could change the world, but now you spend your days worrying about whether the wind machine on the model's hair will get the result you want. You've stopped taking pictures that matter. You sold out,' she finished huskily, the words out before she could stop them.

Instantly his face became closed, his mouth a thin, derisive line. The silence ticked away like a time-bomb. 'Is that what you think, Sam?' His voice was deceptively soft, but his anger was apparent. 'So little of me, hmm? Well, maybe this might change your mind,' and his voice lowered with husky intent as he pushed her into an alcove and up against the wall.

It had been what she'd wanted. A punishing kiss; and yet when it happened she discovered that she didn't want his anger, or his pain.

She wanted the impossible; she wanted his love.

His mouth began its assault, and he pulled her tightly against him, until she could feel every taut sinew and muscle. Her breasts were crushed into his chest; she could feel the hammering of his heart, setting up a primeval duet with her own.

She felt a strange heated response to the pressure of that kiss, and she gave a small, bewildered moan against his mouth, and with that sound everything changed. His anger fled and something else took its place. Something which raced through her own body with fiery, enchanting fingers of flame.

Desire.

A desire which as soon as it was born rocketed straight out of control, so that even though they were in an alcove of a public room where any one of a couple of hundred of photographers could have walked in at any moment and seen them she remained powerless to stop him from what he was doing to her. Powerless to halt the mouth which had moved to the bare flesh at her neck, tracing a sensuous path down to her shoulder, so light a touch that she barely felt it, but it sent out tiny explosions of need to every one of her nerve-endings.

She was powerless to resist the hand which moved in an almost leisurely manner to cup and mould one full and straining breast, his fingers sliding across the thin silk of her dress to rub her nipple softly between thumb and forefinger. Men had tried to touch her before, but never like this; his fingers were trailing irresistible fire, but with such unerring experience that she would not, indeed could not, deny him anything that he wanted from her, and she felt herself blossom and flower beneath his touch, and what had started as a sweet aching deep within her became a moist yearning which demanded instant assuagement.

'Oh.' She gave a breathless sigh.

He moved his mouth from her neck so that it was an inch away from hers. 'You like this, don't you?' he whispered. 'You like me touching you?' And his hand brushed lightly over the other breast.

The eroticism of the unnecessary question as much as the touch itself sent her knees weak and trembling. 'You—know I do.'

'You'd let me make love to you, wouldn't you? Now. Right here.'

The words shocked her, thrilled her. 'I——'

Then without warning he put his hands on her shoulders and moved her away from him, rather in the manner that he'd once removed a drunken Charlotte when she had clung to him like a vine.

Sam stared up at him with dazed, bewildered eyes. All she knew was that she'd tasted heaven, and that now he was glaring down at her, his breathing unsteady, his face harsh once more. The anger was back.

'What—happened?' She sounded like someone who had just fainted.

'What happened was that I kissed you,' he returned grimly, somehow making it sound as though he'd been guilty of a major crime. 'I kissed you as you've been asking to be kissed all night. If I'd known how you'd respond I don't think I'd have risked it—I haven't been tempted to make love in a public place since I left my teens behind. I warned you once before, Sam, that if you turn those big brown eyes on a man long enough he'll only do what comes naturally. Except that with me you may get more than you bargained for. Understand?' he warned softly.

He stared down at her; she was still trembling. 'Let's get out of here,' he said abruptly. 'Before I change my mind.'

She followed him mutely from the room, and, once outside, made her excuses and fled to the powder-room before anyone saw her.

The mirror confirmed her worst fears—her hair was mussed where he'd held her head in his hands, running long fingers through it and somehow turning even her scalp into an erogenous zone. Her face was a deathly white, apart from two high spots of colour which scorched her cheeks, and her lips were unnaturally dark—the colour of ripe blackberries—stained by the pressure of his mouth. Even her—oh, lord—even her breasts looked fuller—her nipples two tumescently hard peaks pushing against the fine material of her dress, shamelessly advertising her arousal.

She shivered, shoving her wrists under an icy jet of water from the tap, willing her pulse to slow down to something approaching normal.

She had to get things into perspective. Firstly, it was perfectly natural for a woman of scant sexual experience to be attracted to a man like Declan. Anyone would. But—Gita or no Gita—she was simply not his type. Several inches too short, and a few curves too many.

And it wasn't *his* fault that she'd been over-reacting to him ever since she'd first gone to work for him. Attacking him professionally was a cheap shot—he was justified in his anger. And she owed it to him to apologise.

With her appearance restored as much as possible—though she couldn't seem to do anything about the flush over her cheekbones—she made her way back into the main banqueting-room.

Declan was sitting at a table set for eight, chatting to a woman she'd never seen before, a woman wearing violet silk dungarees with short, spiky blonde hair and a mischievous smile. She was chuckling at something he'd said. Gita was nowhere to be seen.

He looked up as she entered, his eyes cold, and her heart sank. Damn and damn. He was still angry with her and she couldn't blame him.

She sat next to him and he introduced her to the others on the table, but every single name shot out of her head as soon as she heard it. He spent the first two courses chatting to the blonde, who was called Annie and who was a national sports photographer, his chair pushed slightly back, because his legs were too long for the table to accommodate them comfortably, while Sam stared down into her cold herb soup, wondering why it looked just like pond water.

Some time in between the rack of lamb she couldn't touch and the strawberry tart which made her feel sick just looking at it she managed to get his attention.

'I'm sorry about what happened.'

'Forget it.'

'I mean—I shouldn't have said those things——'

'I said *forget it*,' he said quietly, and she shut up.

They all turned their chairs towards the stage as the awards ceremony began, and everyone's attention was on the stage as they began handing out predictable prizes to noisy applause, but Sam could hardly concentrate— her thoughts were full of the hard-faced man who sat behind her, of what had just taken place between them.

Into the mist of her troubled thoughts seeped a hor-
ribly familiar voice, and Sam looked up to find that Gita
had taken the stage, spotlights transforming the gold
tissue of her gown into a glistering second skin.

Startled, Sam glanced behind her to steal a look at
Declan, but he didn't even notice. He sat unmoving, his
face all harshly defined lines which gave nothing away.

'My friends...' Gita began. She looked round the room
as everyone grew quiet. 'Photography is one of the newer
professions, and much of it is taken for granted. Tonight,
we are making a special award to make sure that one
man's work isn't. Four years ago, there was a war in the
Far East which most of the world would rather forget.
More than most wars, it was bloody and it was pointless.
On the world's stage, politicians seemed powerless to
put an end to it.

'All the more remarkable, really, with just a camera
in his hands, was the contribution of one man.'

She smiled, confident of her timing. 'A man who is
very dear to me...' There was a low buzz of excitement.

'A man who is very dear to me,' she continued, 'took
some of the most emotive photographs ever published.
That man is, as I'm sure you've all guessed, Declan
Hunt. And it is for those photos, and his book *The
Innocents*, that I ask you now, Declan, to step forward
and accept this small——' Her voice died away as she
looked over at their table, a question mark in her eyes,
and Sam spun round to find the chair where he'd been
sitting—empty.

There was another buzz—this time of bewilderment—
and Sam turned to Annie in disbelief. 'Where's Declan?'
she whispered.

Annie smiled a funny kind of smile. 'Crept out, looking like thunder.' She stared at Sam. 'You'd better go up and collect it on his behalf.'

Sam opened her eyes wide in horror. '*Me*?' she gasped. 'I can't do that.'

'Well, somebody's got to do it, and you *are* his escort for the evening, aren't you?'

People were looking over expectantly at their table, and Sam rose to her feet reluctantly, her cheeks going pink as someone, somewhere started clapping and the rest of the audience joined in.

Afterwards, the whole thing seemed like a dream. She couldn't remember what she'd said, or what Gita had said either. The only thing she *did* remember was thinking that Declan Hunt was the rudest, most arrogant man in the world. And of being uncomfortably aware of the reason why he'd left.

The reason he'd left now stood on the stage in front of her, a gleaming, golden and darkly beautiful woman. *That* was why he'd walked out—away from the evocative reminder of how things had once been between them, but were no longer. What had Robin said? 'The war lost him Gita'.

Cruel irony indeed, to have to accept an award for the work which had ultimately lost him the woman presenting it to him.

No wonder he'd cut and run.

CHAPTER SIX

SAM banged loudly on the door, her temper still flaring after a night spent tossing and turning and seething before finally deciding that, Gita or no Gita, it had been damnably rude of him to leave like that.

All right, when she'd left the hotel to hail a taxi she'd discovered that there was a long, low limousine—chauffeur-driven, to boot—which had been left at her disposal, ordered by 'Mr Hunt', she was informed. But, car or no car, there was a principal at stake here—you didn't escort someone somewhere for the evening and then just *dump* them.

And she had no intention of waiting until Monday to give him the award he obviously thought so little of—he could have it today. Wrapped round his head if he wasn't careful.

She banged on the door again. Still no reply.

Cautiously, she tried it, and it opened. He was very cavalier with his security arrangements, she thought fleetingly, before reminding herself that any intruder would probably set a new world land-speed record if confronted with the over six feet of solid muscle which was Declan.

She stepped inside, her face instantly crumpling as she saw the worst.

There was a vast open-plan living area with several doors opening off it. One of the bedroom doors was open and she could see Declan lying awkwardly on a low

83

bed, completely bare to just below the navel, with just some exotically patterned material lying in swaths across his narrow hips.

Sam drew in a deep breath and hurried over to him, the breath leaving her in audible relief as she noted the steady rise and fall of his chest. And *what* a chest, she thought briefly, her eyes resting in amazement on every bronzed, sculpted inch of it. No man had the right to be as gorgeous as Declan was. She dropped the carrier bag to the floor and tried to rouse him.

'Declan! Wake up!' she urged, but there was no response, and, starting to get worried, she crouched down and put her hand on his shoulder, feeling the satiny texture of the skin there, and began to shake him. 'Declan! For God's sake—wake up!'

Two barely visible glints of light emanated from his almost-shut eyes, and before she knew it an arm had snaked around her waist and pulled her down on top of him, and he had neatly turned over so that she found herself lying tangled in his arms, lying underneath him in the most intimate way possible, their bodies glued together as if they'd been lovers. And somehow her skirt had ridden up past her knees and a hard, muscular thigh had been automatically thrust between hers, and oh, it felt like heaven to have that hard pressure at that most intimate part of her body. And she had to get out of here before she gave in to the feeling.

Mentally dousing herself in a torrent of cold water, she glared up at him. 'What do you think you're doing?' she demanded.

'What do *you* think I'm doing?' he drawled lazily.

'I——' She was in danger of kissing his neck, which was temptingly close. 'I don't know.'

'Yes, you do,' he whispered. 'I'm finishing off what we started last night, surely?'

She prayed for strength and wriggled, but only half-heartedly. 'Will you let me go?'

'Moving your hips against me like that is only likely to ensure that I won't,' he murmured, and her eyes widened in shock as she felt his instant arousal against her.

It was exciting, to hear his voice husky, slightly un-steady, low and deep and blatantly sexy. She remem-bered the kiss of the night before and how she had succumbed to it, only now she was in an infinitely more dangerous situation. The only thing that lay beneath her and a naked Declan was the flimsy piece of material, which was doing nothing at all to disguise yet another of his very obvious attributes, which, given her lamen-tably small experience of this kind of thing, *should* have filled her with fright, but in reality filled her with awe and anticipation.

'We've got to stop this right now, Declan,' she said breathlessly, her compliant position beneath him making mockery of her words.

But then, just as she was deciding that if he was going to insist on keeping her there she should just lie back and enjoy it, he removed his thigh from in between hers, removed too the arm which lay with insulting lightness at her waist, and moved off the bed with careless grace, readjusting the knotted fabric at his hip as he did so. It was a type of sarong thing; she'd seen pictures of them— men wore them in the East, and she assumed he must have got into the habit of wearing them when he was working there. The material was thin, almost gauzy, and although there were generous swaths of it its soft folds gave definition to the hard form beneath. It was a garment which, on some men, could have looked almost feminine, except that on Declan it didn't look in the least bit feminine . . .

'You're quite right, Sam,' he said, and gave her a hard, bright look. 'We should.'

She sat up on the bed, her breathing erratic, her skirt all hiked up, now thoroughly ashamed of the capitulation implicit in her behaviour.

'Didn't you ever learn that it's dangerous to leave your front door open all night?' she accused.

'And didn't your mother ever warn you about what could happen if you walk into men's bedrooms?' he parried.

She hurriedly got to her feet, smoothing her skirt down as she did so. 'Unfortunately she only told me what to expect from gentlemen.'

'And I'm no gentleman,' he mocked, and walked out of the room, calling over his shoulder as he did so, 'So tell me, Sam—to what do I owe the pleasure of this early morning visit?'

'You mean apart from the fact that you took me to the awards then left me there?'

'I arranged for a car to be left at your disposal,' came the cool, unperturbed voice from the next room. 'Is that why you're here—to grumble?'

'No, it jolly well isn't!' She picked up the carrier bag and hurried after him through the vast open-plan living-room, and through into a sleek stream-lined kitchen— glad enough for an excuse to lose her embarrassment in rage. 'What about this?' she accused, pulling the heavy silver award out.

He gave it a brief glance then turned back to where he was in the process of grinding coffee beans. 'Oh, that.'

'Yes, *that*!' She put it down on the work surface in front of him. 'Don't you think that it was rude, just to get up and walk out like that? *I* had to go up and collect it for you.'

He gave the glimmer of a smile. 'Fame at last, Sam?'

'Don't be so facetious!' she snapped. 'The point I'm making is——' She halted in accusative mid-flow, momentarily deterred by the glitter of warning in his eyes.

'Yes?' he prompted coolly. 'Just what is the point you're making?'

'I just think it was extremely rude of you just to leave, without even bothering to accept the award graciously.'

'And has it occurred to you just why I *did* leave?' he threw over his shoulder as he went back into the sitting-room, carrying two mugs of coffee.

Oh, God, she thought, following slowly in his wake. She couldn't bear to hear it from his lips, she couldn't. She never wanted to see, hear about or even think about Gita ever again. 'No, it hasn't,' she said stiffly. 'I don't think your personal life is really any concern of mine.'

'But we aren't talking about my *personal* life, are we?' he grated as he turned round to face her. 'We're talking about my professional life, which you *do* seem to be concerned about. For example, your pious little remarks about "selling out".'

'I apologised for that,' she protested.

'But you can't unsay it, can you?' His eyes looked as dark as ink, no trace of blue there now. 'Well, at least you can hear the facts before you sit in judgement. Sit down, Sam—I'll tell you why I didn't accept their damned award.'

He stood, only half-clothed—glorious and arrogantly proud as he stared down at her. Quite suddenly, she realised just where she was and who with. 'I think it's best that I go——'

'Sit *down*!' he ordered fiercely.

Without speaking, she obeyed him, sitting down on a squashy sofa, scarcely noticing that he placed a mugful of coffee down in front of her.

'Shall I tell you about war, Sam? Shall I?'

There was passion about him now. Glittering in his eyes.

'War,' he whispered. 'As the man said—it's bloody and it's unnecessary. It's worse than that—it's sheer hell.'

'You were very brave——' she began.

He shook his head, in a violent movement that looked more like an angry lion tossing its mane. 'I wasn't brave,' he ground out. 'Lying in my protected zone, recording misery. What I did was far worse than what any soldier did.'

She saw the pain etched deep on his features, and felt a sudden and overpowering desire to blot it out. 'What are you talking about?' she said gently.

His eyes flared, bright as beacons. 'Oh, to be a soldier, Sam—at least they were honest; they believed in a cause and they fought for it. Death became duty. But not me.' He gave a bitter laugh. 'Oh, no. Not me. Do you know what I did, Sam? Do you?'

She shook her head. 'Stop it,' she whispered. 'Stop hurting yourself.'

But he raged on quietly as if she hadn't spoken, his eyes boring into her like weapons. 'I sat and watched. Click, click, click. Once, I saw a village being bombed. After the all-clear was given, I went in to take photos.

I stood in the ruins of a house, where a mother cradled her dead child. And——' his voice was a blank, empty thing '—I took photos.'

She felt as though she was encased in ice. 'What happened?'

He pointed to the thin scar down one cheek, the tiny imperfection which failed to mar the exquisite features. 'She lost her head. She was mad with grief, and mad that I'd intruded on it. She came at me, punching, kicking, raking her nails at me. And I let her. Somehow it helped. I gave her everything that was in my wallet, picked up my camera, and left. I took a flight out that week. Sold out and started a fashion studio in New York. So now you know.'

She shook her head. 'I know that photo. Everyone does—and it was that photo which was credited with stopping the war.' She remembered the stark, harrowing depiction of raw, naked grief, the silence it had stunned her into when she'd first seen it. 'It was published on the front cover of nearly every newspaper all over the world. It, more than anything else, brought home to ordinary people the unnecessary brutality of it all. And ordinary people objected.' She remembered the marches, the demonstrations, and the eventual conclusion of the war. 'You couldn't have stopped that baby from being killed, Declan, but by showing it you helped others, you know you did.'

There was a long silence. He drank some coffee, then stared at her for a long, long moment. 'Thanks,' he said, at last. Then, 'I don't want awards for doing my job,' he said quietly. 'Do you understand?'

'Yes.' She did, at last. He was just not that kind of man. He didn't need any of the glittering prizes.

'And if my pictures did any good at all, then so be it. That's why I took them. The war is over. What I don't want is for the people who fought in it, relatives of people who died, to see me in some fancy dinner-jacket in a luxury hotel, tripping up to collect an award at what they will undoubtedly see as some fatuous showbiz occasion.'

He spoke with a quiet, dignified conviction and tears shimmered unexpectedly in the depths of her eyes. 'Oh, God, Declan. Can you ever forgive me for the things I said to you?'

He swore underneath his breath. 'Don't go all helpless on me, Sam.' And then, quite surprisingly, he smiled, and its effect on her was like a body-blow. 'You know I'm a sucker for those big brown eyes of yours, don't you?' he mocked.

I want him to make love to me, she thought suddenly. I want to take the pain away from his face. I want him to fill me, to possess me. If he tries to touch me now, I shan't be able to resist him.

But he didn't try to touch her. Just gave her a smile which her half-crazed brain told her bordered on gentle, though when she thought about it afterwards she realised that it had, in effect, been dismissive.

'I have to go out,' he said.

'I'm sorry, I——'

'I'm taking pictures of your youth centre, remember?'

'Yes. Yes, of course.'

She wanted him to ask her to go with him, to hold his camera, to load his films, to scurry around moving things for him, checking the light. But he didn't. And her reasons for wanting to go were nothing to do with assisting him in his work.

She wanted to go because she was falling in love with him. Deeply, and irrevocably.

A man whom every woman would want, but who seemed still committed to a woman who belonged to someone else.

CHAPTER SEVEN

DECLAN'S photos of the youth club were successful on a scale not dreamed of by any of them.

'You wouldn't think,' said Michael to Sam on the day after publication, 'that pictures of a grotty youth club could have so much clout.' He saw Sam's face. 'Not that I don't think your club is a great place, 'cause I do. It's just——'

'It's because they've hit a nerve with the public,' said Sam slowly, as she spread the newspaper out. 'Declan's done it again.' She looked down once more at the main photo.

Declan had gone national, his pictures of the vandalised club striking a distressing note, while its unlikely inhabitants looked set to become instant stars. People liked seeing these tough nuts from a notorious part of London's inner city playing pool with teenagers unable to get out of the confines of their wheelchairs. And there was a genuine air of affection between all the members, no sense of patronisation from one part of the group towards the other. What Declan had done was somehow to catch the boys and girls doing what they did best—having fun.

'He's so *good*,' said Sam fervently. 'He should be doing this kind of stuff all the time.'

'I should have guessed,' came a dry voice at the door, 'that Sam would have some kind of constructive criticism.'

She whirled round, wishing that she could bite her tongue off as she and Michael followed him into the studio.

'Declan,' he said, 'the paper rang to say that donations for the centre have started to flood in—they're registering with a bank as a national charity. Oh, and the BBC want you to do a three-minute slot at the end of the one o'clock news.'

Declan scowled. 'Tough. Well, Sam'll have to do it.'

He was out of his mind. 'I *can't* do it—I know nothing about television.'

'Keep your eye on the red light and don't smile insincerely, that's all you need to know,' he growled.

'You aren't serious, Declan.'

'I am. If not—get John to do it.'

'John?'

'Yeah. John.'

'John would be hopeless. He mumbles.'

He grinned. 'Oh, you noticed, did you? I don't care who does it, Sam. Anyone you like, but not me.'

'You *have* to do it.'

'*Have* to?' The smile vanished. 'Is that an order?'

She'd overstepped the mark. Again. 'It's you they want,' she pleaded.

'I'm a photographer, not a bloody PR man!'

'Think of all the good you'll do,' she persisted. 'You'll get a much better response than someone nobody's ever heard of. You're a name, Declan, whether you like it or not. *Please.*'

There was a tussle on his face between amusement and irritation, and irritation won. 'OK, I'll do it,' he said grudgingly. 'Now when you've quite finished organising my life for me, perhaps you could see your way to getting your persuasive little person into the dark-room and printing out the contacts I've ringed, which have been sitting in your in-tray since yesterday.'

'Yes, Declan,' she said hastily.

'Next thing——' he turned to Michael '—she'll be getting me to open garden fêtes.'

Sam heard Michael laugh. 'Come off it, Declan, you know you love it really—she's got you eating out of her hand.'

Sam quickly shut the dark-room door as she heard Declan's roared reply.

She was veering from acute joy one moment to gloomy resignation the next. He filled her every waking thought, but she did everything she could to hide it from him, for she suspected that if he guessed she'd be out on her ear. Broken-hearted assistants did not make good assistants, particularly if the target of their unrequited passion worked right alongside them.

OK, he did seem to be *physically* attracted to her sometimes. But only sometimes. And since that morning when she'd gone round to his flat, he had shown nothing but polite indifference towards her.

She sighed as she plunged her prints into the stop-bath, put them in the finish, then set them out to dry.

'Your mother's on the phone,' said a deep voice.

She jumped, the physical reality of him, as always, surpassing her wildest daydreams about him. 'Oh. Thanks. She shouldn't have phoned me at work.'

'No.'

He sounded distinctly unamused, she thought. Which was slightly unreasonable since it was the first call she'd ever received at work.

She picked up the phone. 'Hello, Mother,' she said, trying to inject a little enthusiasm into her voice.

'*Darling*!' The voice dropped conspiratorially. 'That *man*! I couldn't resist ringing you at work; I was dying to speak to him.'

Of course.

'That deep voice would melt an iceberg. Charlotte tells me——' the high, tinkly laugh '—that he's as wonderful in the flesh as in his pictures.'

'Mother, please,' said Sam tonelessly, wishing that Declan would get out of the studio instead of standing right next to her, studying the newly developed prints of the model who had last week rung him up *four* times. There was no guarantee that her mother couldn't be heard. Even so, Sam was surprised. As a famous model in the Sixties, her mother was usually more sophisticated than to behave like a fan over a photographer, famous or not—after all, she'd met enough of them herself in her time. Declan *must* have laid on the charm with a trowel, she thought, eyeing his broad, denim-covered shoulders acidly.

Her mother chattered on inconsequentially before she dropped her bombshell. 'So we're going to see you, I gather.'

'Mother, what *are* you talking about?'

'Well, darling, your nice Mr Hunt tells me that you'll be shooting down in this part of the world next week, and that you'll both call in and see us. I must say, I *am* excited.'

Sam's heart fell. 'I don't know if there'll be enough time,' she said woodenly.

'Well, he seems to think there will. And he *is* the boss, isn't he? Don't be a spoilsport, darling; I hardly ever get to meet any new people these days.' Her mother's voice dropped unconsciously. 'He says that you'll be renting a cottage. I suppose it'll be—you know—*all right*. Your staying with him.'

Sam could hardly believe her ears. *Staying* with him? This was news to her. Her heart leapt into beats that were way out of control, but her voice remained calm. 'Mother, I *am* twenty-six years old. I do know how to look after myself.'

'I know, darling—but you don't know very much about men, and, well—that particular man... Still, he isn't likely to be interested in you, is he?'

Sam didn't know whether to laugh or cry at her mother's unconscious cruelty. She replaced the handset to find a pair of narrowed navy eyes arrowed in her direction.

'Why did you tell my mother we'd call in to see them?'

He shrugged. 'I told her we'd be down in their part of the world—we can easily make a short detour and drop in and see them.'

'Nice of you to ask me,' she returned sarcastically.

He gave her a curious look. 'Don't you like your mother, Sam?'

'That's none of your business!'

He shrugged. 'No, you're right, it isn't,' he returned in a bored voice. 'I couldn't care less whether we go or not; I just thought you might like to. Ring them back and cancel. Do any damn thing you like, only keep me out of it—I've had about as much of you as I can take today.'

The atmosphere between them was strained for the next few days; Declan was positively taciturn and nothing she said seemed to please him. If she tried to be especially nice—a bit of a creep, if she was honest—then he snapped at her, until, bitten once too often, she snapped back. And then he glowered at her as if she didn't know her place!

He had her tied up in emotional knots. It was a terrible feeling, yearning for someone who was so out of reach, particularly as she'd had a brief and tantalising taste of just how shattering his lovemaking would be. Far better for Sam if he'd never touched her. What you'd never had, you never missed...

She found that she'd completely lost interest in food—she didn't even seem to *feel* hungry any more and for the first time in her life she lost weight without even trying.

And what was even worse was that Sam walked into the studio a couple of days after the awards to find Declan and Michael huddled over a newspaper.

It transpired that Gita had decided to do an interview for a tabloid entitled 'Gita's private album', which managed to include several old photographs of her with Declan. Sam felt quite sick with jealousy as she saw a much younger, softer, laughing Declan—none of the harshness on his face then—with Gita, hair loose like a wraith, staring up at him with frank adoration on her face.

'Declan's *furious*,' confided Michael later as they shared a plate of salad sandwiches. 'He hates publicity about his private life.'

'I wonder what made her do it?' said Sam, absently sliding a piece of cucumber into her mouth.

'He rang her and asked just that.'

'He *rang* her?'

Michael's eyebrows rose at the sharpness of her tone. 'Sure. Why shouldn't he?'

Why *shouldn't* he? Because I want him, thought Sam fiercely. I want him so much that it's unbearable. 'What did Gita say?' she asked tonelessly.

Michael shrugged. 'Just that she needed the publicity for some new charity she's chairing and couldn't see that it could do any harm.'

Not harm, perhaps—but bittersweet heartache for Declan to be reminded of what were obviously happy times.

He did the short interview for the BBC. Michael and Sam closed the studio for half an hour and went to the local TV shop to watch it.

Declan's face filled the screen, larger than life—and twice as good-looking, thought Sam wistfully.

'Now there's something I wouldn't mind finding at the foot of my bed on Christmas morning,' sighed the salesgirl.

The interviewer was female, given to leaning across towards him to make her point.

'Mr Hunt,' she began 'there is a school of thought which believes that inactivity breeds crime. Do you believe that the youth of this country are adequately catered for?'

'Certain sections, yes. But not all.'

'So your photos were really making a political point?'

He gave the interviewer a look of barely concealed impatience. 'I am a photographer, Miss Stapps, not a politician.'

'Yet your war photos caused a political storm at the time...'

'I take photos,' he said carefully. 'The public interpret them. How they choose to do so is a matter for their own consciences.'

She tried a different tack. 'So are we to take it that these portraits of an inner-city youth club mark your departure from the world of high fashion and a return to photo journalism as Gita—Lady Squires—hinted on breakfast television this morning?'

In the television shop, fifty screens carried an image of Declan smiling the most gritted smile that Sam had ever seen.

'No comment,' he remarked.

He returned from the TV studios that afternoon in a poorly disguised temper, and then, to her horror, having left the door of the dark-room open, she heard him telephoning Gita and arranging to meet her...

The following afternoon, Bob, her brother-in-law, rang to say he was working late and staying over in town and could they meet for dinner?

Sam was hesitant, but Bob was insistent.

'*Please*,' he said. 'I need to talk to you about Charlotte. We're going through a bad patch, Sam.'

So what else was new? 'All right,' sighed Sam. 'What time?'

'I'll pick you up at eight.'

It was unfortunate that it was a night when Declan had worked her late—having her develop some prints of breathtaking simplicity for him—and, consequently, she was running behind time, and said so.

'Youth centre tonight, then?' he asked.

'Actually, no. I happen to be going out for dinner.'

'For *dinner*? Who with?'

She didn't like the note of surprise in his voice. She might not be in Gita's class, but she wasn't exactly Attila the Hun. And she didn't like his presumptuous question, either. She remembered his phone call to Gita and was deliberately evasive. 'Just a—friend,' she said coolly.

Unfortunately, he uncharacteristically insisted on giving her a lift home to her flat, and he took the worst possible route which meant that they got snarled up in the traffic, so that by the time they arrived Bob was already there, leaning against his silver BMW, his tall, blond good looks exciting the interest of two women walking down the street.

A nerve worked in Declan's cheek as he brought the black Porsche to a halt. Sam saw Bob's eyes narrow as he mentally priced the car.

'That's who you're having dinner with?' he asked quietly. 'Your brother-in-law? How cosy.'

Sam's cheeks flamed, knowing what he must be thinking, but *damn* him—it was no worse than he had done. At least there was nothing between her and Bob, which was more than could be said about Declan and Gita.

So, her conscience clear, she stared back frostily at his censorious expression.

'It is,' she agreed sweetly. 'Very cosy. Would you like to meet him?'

His mouth twisted. 'No, thanks.' He leaned across her and opened the door. 'Have fun,' he said softly, his eyes glittering with some strange, warning message, and Sam swallowed quickly as she stepped out of the car.

Fun it most certainly wasn't. According to Bob, he and Charlotte had been fighting non-stop. Sam tried her best to provide a sympathetic yet impartial ear, but she was glad when the evening was over and she could escape to her flat.

But sleep was a long time coming as she lay in bed, unable to rid herself of the memory of Declan's darkly disapproving face as he'd driven away.

CHAPTER EIGHT

DECLAN was cool towards her for the rest of the week.

Sam was dreading the location trip with him in this kind of mood. *And* she had the visit to her parents to contend with. She had managed to condense it into tea, since tea seemed the shortest and most innocuous meal to attend, and at least Flora would be there.

They were travelling down to Sussex just before noon, would stop for lunch on the way, and arrive at her parents' at around tea-time.

Declan had hired a cottage close to a sandy cove for the shoot. The two models and the art director would be joining them the next day, by which time Declan and Sam would have worked out all the best locations.

And if Declan had been cool all week, Sam had been jumpy. The thought of spending a whole night alone in a country cottage with Declan filled her with feelings which ranged from acute shyness through to a deep, pounding excitement, before she silently warned herself against raising any hopes which were only likely to be dashed.

Declan collected her promptly and the drive was punctuated with snapped questions which made her feel as though she were on the witness stand.

'Do you want to lunch here?' He slowed the car as they drove through a sleepy village.

'I don't mind.'

'Is that a yes or a no?'

'Yes.'

It was a meal wasted. Sam picked at a prawn salad, watching while Declan tucked into a fish pie with alacrity.

'For God's sake—eat something,' he said. 'I told you before that you don't need to lose any weight.'

'I'm just not hungry,' she said truthfully, then, not so truthfully, 'I had a big breakfast.'

As they approached the grey stone house of her parents, she unconsciously sank further into her seat.

The front door was opened by her mother.

Age had not diminished what had once been sensational good looks—Jayne Gilbert was still a beautiful woman—but Sam privately thought that she should try a little less hard to look like a thirty-year-old, and instead just be what she was—a very attractive fifty-five-year-old.

Mrs Gilbert put her head to one side to study the tall man at her daughter's side and smiled. 'Declan.' She said his name as though he were a long-lost friend. 'May I call you that? I feel I know you already, Sam's told us *so* much about you!'

Which was frankly untrue, thought Sam, her heart sinking as she watched her mother flirting like mad. She had told them nothing about Declan, not a thing.

He smiled. 'Sure. I'm very pleased to meet you, Mrs Gilbert.'

'Call me Jayne.' Her eyes flicked over her daughter. 'Hello, darling.' She offered a pale, fragrant cheek. 'Been dieting? It's an improvement, I must say. Do come in— Charlotte and Bob are already here. Come with me, Declan.' She linked her arm through his and smiled up at him in the manner of Scarlett O'Hara looking up at

Rhett. 'It's a while since I had such a handsome man on my arm.'

Sam's heart sank as she followed them inside, wondering if Declan was going to fall for her mother's spiel, or, worse still, her sister's.

The group was assembled awkwardly in the sitting-room. Sam kissed her long-suffering father, and introduced Declan to him. Bob was also introduced—a brief flash of recognition lighting his eyes as he recognised the driver of the very expensive Porsche. Charlotte sat curled up on the floor, looking as lovely as ever, her fine bones and porcelain flesh clearly defined in the bright light which flooded in through the windows. Today, she was wearing a very short black Lycra skirt with a black polo-neck sweater over it which provided a gleaming backdrop for the moon-pale blonde hair which fell to her fashionably tiny breasts. If only, thought Sam, she'd looked a bit more like Charlotte, instead of inheriting all her looks from her father, much though she loved him.

'Hello, Sam,' said Charlotte.

They didn't touch. 'Hello,' said Sam. 'Where's Flora?' She looked in vain for Charlotte's face to light up at the mention of her only child.

'Upstairs. She insisted on preparing a surprise for you—God knows what.'

At that moment they heard the unmistakable sounds of a child bounding downstairs, two at a time, and an enthusiastic bundle ran across the room and hurled herself into Sam's arms.

'Aunty Sammie, Aunty Sammie! I've drawn you a picture!' And then she went enchantingly pink. 'Hello, Declan,' she said shyly.

'Hello, Flora,' he smiled. 'Taken any good pictures lately?'

Flora cast a hurried glance at her mother. 'I haven't got my own camera—yet.'

Dark brows were delicately knitted together. 'I can see that we shall have to remedy that, won't we?' he said casually. 'Remember that roll of film you took of Sam?'

'Yes! Did you develop it?'

'Sure did. Printed it, too. Here.' And he pulled a small brown envelope from his faded flying jacket and tossed it to the excited child.

Sam looked up and met his eyes in surprise as Flora eagerly spilled the black and white prints all over the carpet in her haste to show them round.

'Oh, *Dec-lan*,' said Charlotte huskily. 'You're spoiling her.'

'But that's what little girls are for, surely—to be spoiled?'

Sam shot him a grateful glance. It had been a thoughtful gesture of his.

She bent down to tickle her niece's neck. 'Now then,' she asked. 'Where's this picture you've drawn for me?'

The picture was picked up and deposited on Sam's lap immediately.

'Careful, Flora,' said Bob stiffly. 'Sam doesn't want to be covered in felt-tip.'

Sam glared at him over her niece's head. 'I don't mind. It's only an old sweater.' Her voice softened. 'It's a gorgeous picture, darling. Who's this—you?'

'Yes—me in the blue frock you made for me last Christmas—there's the bow. And that's the pram——'

Sam looked into her niece's unusual golden eyes. 'Pram? Whose pram—dolly's pram?'

'Not dolly's. Mummy's.'

'I'm pregnant,' said Charlotte flatly.

'Oh!' Sam smiled, a little uncertainly. 'Congratulations—you must be very happy.'

'Bob is.' Charlotte gave her husband a petulant smile. 'Aren't you, darling?'

'You know I am,' her husband replied gruffly.

Charlotte then turned to Declan who was now, Sam noticed, reclining quietly in a chair, watching all the goings-on with interest. 'I hate being pregnant,' she said moodily. 'It's awful for a woman when she loses her figure.'

'Really?' he said politely.

She looked at him from beneath her lashes. It was, thought Sam, the only way she knew how to look at a man.

'It's dreadful,' reiterated Charlotte. 'I mean—I'm twelve weeks now, and I feel so *fat*.'

Eyes were drawn, as they were intended to be drawn, to the reed-like slimness of her figure. Sam glanced over at Declan, but to her surprise he was not looking at Charlotte at all, but had started talking to her father about local land prices.

'Will you help me make tea, Sam?' asked Charlotte pointedly.

'OK.' Sam stood up. 'But after tea I'm going to thrash my niece at draughts—that is, if she still plays.'

'Oh, yes.' Flora dimpled at Declan. 'Aunty Sammie taught me. She sometimes lets me win,' she confided.

'Not today,' promised Sam with a twinkle in her eye, and followed her sister out into the kitchen like a lamb to the slaughter.

Charlotte plugged in the kettle then turned to face Sam, leaning back against the sink as she did so, a calculating look in her eyes.

'Well?' she asked. 'Has he broken your heart yet?'

Years of childhood squabbles could never quite be shrugged off, and Sam took refuge, as she had always done, in procrastination. 'Who?'

'Oh, don't be so obtuse,' Charlotte snapped. 'Him. Wonderboy.'

'He's the man I work for,' said Sam carefully. 'Nothing more than that.'

'You can't fool me,' said Charlotte heatedly. 'I know you too well. I saw the way you were looking at him. But let me give you a word of advice, Sam. Men like that will always have women looking at them like that. Women who will give them whatever they want to take, women more beautiful than you by far. And all he'd have to do is snap his fingers.'

She smiled suddenly, and Sam recognised the smile instantly. It was the same smile she had once used to charm their mother to let her have the extra treat, the trip to town, the first dip into the dressing-up box. It was the same smile she had used when she'd told Sam she was going to be married . . .

'Tell me, have you slept with him yet?'

Sam eyed her coldly, her distaste mingling with shock as she suddenly realised that Charlotte was *jealous*, jealous of *her*, her small, insignificant sister. She wouldn't have been human if she hadn't known a few seconds of sweet revenge, before she remembered that Charlotte's fears were groundless.

Maybe once, in a mad moment, Declan had desired her, but his behaviour towards her over the past days had shown her that that was an aberration he had no intention of repeating. However, the last person she was going to tell *that* to was Charlotte.

'Have you?' repeated her sister slyly.

'That's surely none of your business,' snapped Sam.

Charlotte had the grace to look abashed. 'Perhaps it isn't. But let me give you a word of advice, as one woman to another. Don't go to bed with him. You'll only regret it in the long run.'

'I shall do as I damned well please,' answered Sam defiantly.

'Are you baking cakes out here, or making tea?' drawled a deep voice, and Sam whirled round in horror to find Declan's long, muscular shape draped casually in the doorway of the kitchen.

Good grief—how much had he heard? Part of her answer to Charlotte had been bravado, but only part, and Declan would be horrified if he thought that she was discussing him in such coldly clinical terms, as though he were some kind of stud.

'Oh, Declan,' smiled Charlotte prettily as she tipped boiling water into the teapot. 'You're just in time to carry the tray.'

They drank tea and ate angel cake, and at least then Sam was able to sit down at the small table in the window and play games of draughts with Flora, which became increasingly uproarious as her father stood behind his granddaughter and helped her to win time and time again.

But the atmosphere was never easy, and, much as she was sad to say goodbye to Flora, Sam was glad to escape from the cloying environment of her parents' home. If only she didn't feel so ridiculously nervous at the thought of being alone with Declan. Working with him was one thing, but staying overnight with him . . .

She made a few banal attempts to talk about the passing scenery, hoping that he might join in and dispel some of her anxieties, but he didn't. Indeed, he was almost completely silent on the journey to the cottage, and in the end Sam ending up joining in and saying nothing.

Indeed, he waited until they had dragged both their suitcases inside, turned on the electricity, and he had lit a fire against the chill in the air which had descended. He waited until then before he turned round and fixed her with his most penetrating stare, and said, 'So are you going to tell me about it?'

CHAPTER NINE

SAM stared at Declan. 'Tell you about what?'

He looked at her. 'About why your brother-in-law spends most of the time being so morose, about why your sister speaks to you so appallingly, and why you let her. The atmosphere in there today was electric. Tell me, Sam—does Charlotte know about these cosy little dinners you share with her husband?'

She glared at him, bitterly hurt by his implication, and something inside her snapped. 'It's dinner in the singular, not the plural, if you must know,' she said icily. 'And I'm sure that Bob told Charlotte.'

His mouth gave a little twist at this. 'Then I apologise,' he said abruptly.

She nodded, registering as she did so the total silence outside the cottage. She gave a nervous laugh. 'It's funny. We seem to spend an awful lot of time apologising to each other.'

He gave her another swift stare. 'So we do. And what do you think that tells us?'

She shrugged. 'That we argue a lot.'

'So we do.' Then he laughed. 'Life with you is never easy, Sam, but it sure as hell ain't dull!' He turned and walked to the cabinet which stood in one corner of the room. 'Do you want a drink?'

In the mood she was in she felt as though she could down a bottle of Scotch in one. 'I'll have one if you're having one.'

He smiled. 'Undoubtedly.'

She was pleased when he opened some red wine, poured out two glasses and brought them to place them on the stone hearth in front of the fire.

'Come and sit down here,' he invited.

She went forward hesitantly, like a bird sensing a cat, took the glass and sat down. 'I don't really want to talk about it.'

'Yes, you do,' he contradicted. 'Drink your wine.'

The wine helped, but the moment she'd drunk half the glass she immediately regretted it, because she was so tempted to confide in him. The fire, the wine, the presence of the strong man she so admired and was falling in love with—all these combined to lull her into a state of dreamy well-being. It was the kind of scenario which took place only in the setting of her wildest imaginings, and yet now here it was—happening in real life.

'Talking helps.' He watched her from beneath the dark lashes.

'Does it?'

'Yes, sometimes.'

And then she remembered how he'd unburdened himself to her, told her all about the war. She had been surprised by his frankness. What harm could it do? She sipped her wine. 'Bob was my boyfriend first, years ago.'

He nodded, running a long finger round the rim of his wine glass, saying nothing.

She sighed. 'Oh, it all goes back much further than that, really. Charlotte was always the favoured child, the image of my mother, whereas I was always the tomboy—stolid, reliable old Sam.'

'Sam and Charlotte,' he mused. 'But do they never call you Samantha, or her Charlie?'

Sam sipped her wine. 'No fear. Mother had decided on the names beforehand—we were to be called after her two greatest modelling friends, and apparently, when I arrived, she said to Charlotte, "Oh, dear, this one looks a real little bruiser—we'll have to call her Sam." And it stuck. It's suits me,' she said defiantly. 'Samanthas are beautiful and graceful, not small and——'

'Feisty?' he suggested.

'Not me,' she said firmly.

'So tell me about Bob. And Charlotte.'

She shrugged. 'It's the classic story. Bob liked to ride, and so did I. When I was a kid he used to let me tag along, and I helped him on his parents' farm. I guess that for a long time I hero-worshipped him.'

'And what was Charlotte doing all this time?'

'Oh, Charlotte was three years older than me, and had much bigger fish to fry. She used to date all the "right" people—you know, the brigadier's son, people like that. There was even a viscount, though he was years older.'

'But she didn't marry any of them?' he probed.

She shook her head. 'No, she didn't. Charlotte wasn't out of the correct drawer for any of the men she dated.'

'Or maybe no one fell in love with her?' he suggested softly.

She stared at him in disbelief. 'Charlotte's the kind of woman whom men go ga-ga about,' she said, trying to keep the bitterness out of her voice.

'Initially, perhaps. She has a certain gloss of appeal which some men would undoubtedly go for, but men generally want more than just the pretty packaging for a lifetime partner.'

It was inconceivable to think of Charlotte in these terms; he was just being kind, trying to make her feel better.

He stared at her. 'Carry on,' he said in a low voice. 'With your story.'

She stared back in confusion. Declan was a strong and powerful man—by rights he shouldn't be interested in the trivial squabbles of her family—and yet she found it amazingly easy to tell him things which she forced herself to forget over the years. She gave a little shrug. 'Like Mummy, she went into modelling—well, you already knew that—you worked with her, didn't you?'

'Once or twice,' he answered, non-committally.

'She wanted to break into films, really make the big time, but it never happened.'

He nodded, like one familiar with the aspirations of beautiful women. 'Have some more wine.'

She let him fill her glass. So what was it—the wine making her speak so freely, or the soft concern she imagined she saw written in his eyes?

'Charlotte moved to London, and my friendship with Bob grew into something more than that. I started seeing him...' She looked up, biting her lip. 'Funny expression, isn't it? We started dating on my sixteenth birthday. He wanted to get married when I reached eighteen—I know how old-fashioned that sounds——'

He shook his head. 'Not at all.'

Like hell! His polite rejoinder brought her to her senses—what was she doing pouring her heart out to a sophisticated man of the world like Declan?

'Don't stop now,' he said softly.

Oh, why not? cried a lonely voice inside her—she'd come so far now. 'Then, one weekend, Charlotte came home unexpectedly.' She could remember how it had been as though it were yesterday. Charlotte, pale-faced and wearing faded jeans, looking just like a fallen angel, giving Bob that slow, steady smile, and Bob staring at her, transfixed, like a man who had just glimpsed paradise. 'Oh, I don't really blame Bob—she was even more beautiful then, just like a flower, really. At first I didn't twig what was going on. I mean, Bob cancelled a couple of things, but that was nothing new, because the farm often took up a lot of time. And then I found out—just a malicious whisper or two. I confronted Bob, and he admitted it, said they'd been seeing one another, told me that it had all been a big mistake, but by then it was too late, and Charlotte was pregnant——'

'But not by Bob, I think?'

It was as though he had plucked the thought from her mind, had had the temerity to voice the guilty suspicion she had fostered for all these years but never dared to discuss with anyone. She rounded on him. 'Don't you ever dare say a thing like that.' Her voice shook with quiet rage.

He remained unperturbed, the blue eyes dark and steady. 'But why not, when we both know it's true?'

'You can't know anything——'

'I know what I see. I see an unhappy child both of whose parents resent her. A child, nevertheless, who looks nothing like either parent——'

'But that often happens!' she protested. 'Children develop traits from their ancestors and——'

'So that's what they say, is it?' he said softly. 'Is that what they tell you?'

The soft words were her undoing. She found herself blinking furiously. 'I'm sorry,' she said, in a low voice. 'I've never talked about it like that before. The irony is that—that——' But not that. She couldn't tell him that.

He threw a log on to the fire and it fizzed orange and gold immediately. 'It may not be so bad between them, now that she's pregnant again. She may give him the son all farmers seem to want. But the marriage was probably doomed from the start, based as it was on lies.' His mouth tightened. 'Lies don't make sound foundations.'

He sounded very bitter, and Sam wondered if he was thinking of Gita. Was he sitting there wishing that Gita would end her marriage, because wasn't that, too, based on a lie? She had married Robin for all the wrong reasons, to gain a title—Robin himself had told her that. And it was obvious to anyone that she was still in love with Declan. Was he waiting for her to have the courage to break free from her cage of a marriage so that she could at last be reunited with him? The thought hurt more than it should have done, far more, and to her consternation the blinking was no longer enough to keep the tears at bay, and she helplessly turned her head away as they began to slide down her cheeks.

He said nothing but turned her face back towards him, studying her wet cheeks for a long moment, then he leaned forward and gathered her in his arms as if she'd been Flora herself, pulling her into his chest and smoothing her hair down with long, rhythmical movements.

'Did he hurt you?' he muttered into her hair. 'Did he hurt you very much?'

She couldn't speak, the emotion of all she'd just told him overwhelming her like a huge tidal wave.

But as the tears began to subside, she discovered that Bob was the last thing on her mind. It was Declan who filled her thoughts like an addiction. These were Declan's arms holding her tightly against him, so tightly that she could hear the pounding of his heart, steady and strong and insistent, like the relentless beat of waves against the sand. Declan's breath, warm against her neck.

Declan, whom I love, she thought, acknowledging the impossible with calm acceptance.

Quite without thinking, because it suddenly seemed the most natural thing in the world, she reached her arms up around his neck, and the movement brought them even closer, so that her breasts were crushed against him, and she pressed them even closer, quite by instinct, loving the feel of his heat burning into her like a brand.

He stared down at her for a long moment, his eyes narrowed so that they looked like nothing but glittering shards of some mysterious metal, but even so she could see the raw desire written there, and the pulse hammering at the base of his throat like a drum beating out its hunger for her.

She made a little sigh of anticipation, her arms tightening around his neck, her hips moving in unconscious invitation, and his eyes became suddenly fierce.

'No,' he said in a voice quiet with some suppressed emotion which she took to be anger. 'I'm not going to make love to you, Sam. That's taking comfort a little too far—wouldn't you say?'

She stared at him blankly. He meant...it was a mocking reprimand, she realised numbly. He had been comforting her in her distress, nothing more; it had been *she* who had tried to take it further—offering herself to a man who had no intention of making love to her. Why couldn't she just accept that? Shame made hot colour flare up, burning across her cheekbones, and he saw it, and his mouth twisted into a tight, derisory slash.

Stiffly, her face set into a tight mask which concealed her shattered pride, she rose to her feet, too.

'You'd better unpack,' he ordered. 'And get an early night. We've a long day ahead of us tomorrow.'

And an even longer night.

She made to leave without speaking but he caught her arm, the contact searing through her like a bushfire. She flinched at the ease with which he could physically control her, and he saw her mouth move, and dropped his hand immediately.

'I'll sort us out something to eat,' he said, glancing at the watch which gleamed gold against his tanned wrist. 'I'll call you when it's ready.'

She shook her head. She would rather starve than endure eating with him after what had just happened. She wanted to be as far away from him as possible. 'I'm not hungry,' she said stubbornly.

'Well, I am, and you must be, too. You left most of your lunch, didn't touch a thing at your parents'. I don't intend for you to have a fainting attack on me tomorrow. Understand?'

Her eyes flashed answering sparks. 'You can't force me to eat, Declan!' she declared.

'Want to bet?' he responded mockingly.

She set her mouth into a straight line and made for her room, not trusting herself to reply, hating herself for virtually offering herself to him, hating him far more for flinging that offer back in her face.

I love him, she thought desperately, and yet I could do physical violence to him. Because he doesn't love me back, that's why.

She stuffed sweaters and jeans into several of the drawers, hardly noticing the pleasing simplicity of the small, clean room, with the blue vase of cornflowers which stood on the dresser and matched the throw-over bedcover, and the curtains which billowed around a window looking directly out to sea.

Declan opened some tins and they ate their meal mainly in silence. Declan was polite, but distant, withdrawn into that same enigmatic shell she'd first grown used to at the studio, and Sam responded in kind, forcing replies she hoped didn't sound forced, not wanting him to know how much his rejection of her had hurt.

'Wine?' he asked.

She shook her head. She'd had enough wine earlier; perhaps if she hadn't she might not have made such a colossal fool of herself. 'Just coffee, thanks. I'll make it. Would you like some?'

'Please.'

It was unnerving to clatter around the kitchen knowing that his eyes were on her. She thought how bizarre it would look to an outsider, this curiously domestic scene: the man with the shadowed moody face leaning back in his chair, long legs draped carelessly in front of him, while the small woman with the strained, pale face strove to make a jug of coffee without revealing her shaking hands.

But when it was made she could stand no more; picking up her steaming mug, she walked past him.

'I'm going to turn in now,' she said stiffly. 'Goodnight.'

'I shan't be long myself. Goodnight, Sam.'

It sounded so final, like goodbye.

CHAPTER TEN

THE cry sounded unnaturally loud in the stillness of the night, and Sam sat bolt upright in bed, her hand clasped instinctively over her thudding heart while she listened.

And then she heard it again. A man's cry.

Declan's cry.

Without stopping to think she leapt from the bed, slithering into the scarlet satin pyjamas she had not bothered to put on last night when she'd finally gone to bed, unwilling to do more than crawl miserably underneath the covers and pray for a sleep which had been a long time in coming.

She ran along the short corridor to Declan's room, hesitating only for a second before she put her hand on the handle of the closed door.

As soon as she pushed the door open, she could see that he was sitting up in bed—not asleep, yet not awake—in the grip of some awful nightmare, and his hoarse, wordless exclamation of despair tore at her heart.

'Declan!'

The duvet was on the floor, and he wore another of those exotic pieces of material knotted just below his navel. She ran to his side, and did what came as naturally to her as breathing—she pulled him to her and wrapped her arms round him and cradled his dark head against her beating heart.

The cry became a shuddering breath.

'Declan,' she urged softly. 'It's all right.'

She sensed that he had woken from the dream, could tell by the subtle alteration of his breathing, but he didn't move, and neither did she. She could have gone on holding him like that all night.

She didn't care how he would choose to interpret it, for at that moment he needed her, as troubled men had needed women to hold them in their arms since battles had begun. She found herself speaking softly, bending her head a little so that her mouth was close to his ear, the resonance low-pitched so that it should soothe him.

'It's all right. You were having a bad dream.' She felt the warmth of his breath through the silky fabric of her pyjama jacket. 'Do you have them very often?'

'Very rarely. Now.'

That last word spoke volumes, and she increased her embrace, her arms tightening protectively, and as she did so he seemed to regain his normal aplomb. He lifted his head and moved a little away from her and looked down into her face.

'Thanks.' He gave a half-smile. 'Did anyone ever tell you you'd make a great nurse?'

'Can't stand the sight of blood——' she started, and could have kicked herself, as she remembered the war-torn source of his nightmares. 'Oh, Declan—I'm sorry——'

He shook his head, leaned over to the locker, and snapped the light on. 'Don't be ridiculous. I'm not made of glass.'

Anything but. Her attention was focused suddenly on the bare torso, all warm, living flesh. She dropped her hands awkwardly.

'I'd better go.' So why did she stay sitting?

'Yes.' And why did he?

'You must be sleepy.'

'Not remotely.'

'Declan, I——'

'Sam.' He said her name with his familiar deep, mocking drawl, but she sensed the urgency behind it. 'I'm doing my best not to start making love to you, but I'm afraid there's only so much I can stand. So will you please go back to your bedroom? Now.'

Some force, far stronger than pride or reason, compelled her to ask, 'Do you want me to?'

Harshly, 'No.'

Her eyes widened. They asked him a question.

When he spoke there was a kind of desperation to his voice. 'For God's sake, Sam—I've been telling myself for weeks now to leave well alone. Sex and work are incompatible. I know that.'

She swallowed. He was thinking of Gita. 'Declan——' It came out like a little prayer, and she heard him utter a curse softly beneath his breath.

'But damn you!' he muttered. 'I've wanted you so badly all day, all week—do you know that?'

'No, I didn't. You certainly didn't show it,' she answered drily, and as she saw him smile a delicious feeling of expectation began to steal over her.

'That's because I've been fighting it,' he muttered, his eyes glittering. 'Fighting you.' His gaze swept lingeringly over the length of her body, a feral gleam lighting his secretive blue eyes. 'God, I want you,' he said deliberately.

His glaring desire flooded her with sweetest confidence, so much that she trembled, and she knew that if she reached out a hand to touch the bare skin of his chest he too would tremble.

'I want you,' he said again, his voice deep and soft.

'Snap,' she whispered, her voice soft and unsteady with excitement.

His mouth curved into a lazy smile. 'Do you?'

Her whole body was crying out for him. The game was unbearably exciting. 'Yes.'

'Convince me,' he commanded softly.

She slowly leaned forward, her mouth staying just a hair's breadth away from his. It was the ultimate in provocation, she realised, her lips curving into a secret smile as she saw the look on his face. 'Like this?' she whispered.

They stayed like that for seconds, frozen in time, prolonging the delicious agony of anticipation. It was as tantalising as the smell of coffee, almost to be kissing when they both wanted to kiss so much, and she wondered who would be the first to crack, surprised and delighted that it should be him, as, with a small groan of surrender, he pulled her into his arms and crushed his mouth down on hers, in total command now.

She went up in flames, dissolving into liquid desire as those hard lips parted hers with their sweet pressure. She found her tongue mimicking the seductive movements of his, exploring his mouth with slow, disbelieving enjoyment; tasting him. And she felt an agonisingly pleasurable ache between her legs, as she pressed herself still closer, wishing that her satin pyjamas would disappear, as if by magic.

Her breasts tingled. She wanted to feel his hands on them. She wanted him to touch every centimetre of her body; she wanted to offer him everything.

'Oh, Declan,' she whispered.

His hands had been framing her face, but now he moved them, one now supporting the small of her back as he pulled her down on to the bed beside him, the other moving beneath the satin of her jacket. His hand stayed poised above a breast which felt tight and full, his movement mimicking the delayed gratification of her kiss, and this time it was she who broke, arching her back up so that her nipple grazed against his palm, and he gave a soft laugh as he captured the whole straining mound, the other hand moving from behind her to begin to undo her jacket.

'I want to see your body,' he whispered, and she froze, imagining his disappointment when he compared her to the stream of beautiful women who had found their way into his bed. Countless models.

She shifted uncomfortably. 'Can you turn the light out?' she whispered nervously.

He stopped unbuttoning, his eyes going from her breasts to her eyes, narrowing in question. 'You prefer it that way, do you, Sam?' he whispered suggestively in her ear. 'That's fine by me. But next time I get to choose.'

Oh, God, she prayed, as she understood his words. He thinks I *know*. Please let me be good for him. Please, please, please. Don't let me disappoint him.

'Sweetheart...' his voice was gently remonstrative '...*relax*.'

She wondered, slightly hysterically, whether he called them all 'sweetheart', or did some merit a 'honey', or even a 'darling'? But then his hands had moved back sweetly to caress her breasts, and all her doubts fled like puffs of smoke on the wind.

'You have beautiful breasts,' he murmured, touching them until she was sure she was going to cry out with pleasure. And then, quite without warning, his dark head moved so that his lips were against her nipples, and he opened his mouth and his tongue began to lick slowly at each engorged tip in turn, and then she *knew* that she was going to cry out. She did.

'Oh ... Declan.'

'You like that, don't you?' he murmured.

'Oh, yes.'

'Do you like this, too?' His hand trailed a slow path down. She sucked her stomach in immediately, and his middle finger found its way to her belly-button. 'Breathe out,' he teased her softly, then murmured, 'You have a beautiful stomach, too.'

'*Declan*!' The hand had captured far more intimate quarry now.

'What?' He moved his fingers luxuriously against her, finding her hotly and moistly inviting.

She felt as though she was going out of her mind. 'It's so—so——'

'I know, sweetheart. I know.' He kissed her deeply, savagely, completely—then, with a sudden movement, he stopped, raising his head and gripping her by the shoulders, so that his eyes dazzled inches away, burning, boring into her as she stared back at him in helpless wonder. In the dim moonlight, his eyes raked over her, at her slender legs, which curved through the satin of her pyjamas, at the opened jacket which exposed the rosy points of her swollen breasts.

'Sit up,' he instructed.

Blood pounding in her head, she did so, and he slipped the jacket off her shoulders, so that she was clad in just the satin trousers.

'Lie down again,' he whispered.

I'm his concubine, she thought dreamily as she obeyed him, watching as he knelt over her to slide the trousers down over her feet and to drop them casually over the side of the bed, as if he had all the time in the world.

'Now...' he gave her a sweet, seductive smile as his hand moved enticingly to the knot of fabric at his hips '...shall I do this? Or would you like to?'

She closed her eyes quickly, afraid that he would see her sudden shyness. 'You.'

The moonlight was nothing like as illuminating as the bedside lamp, but, even so, it revealed quite enough. Excitement and fear thundered in her blood as she opened her eyes a fraction.

'You're peeping, Sam,' he murmured.

And then the wrap fluttered to the floor, and oh, heavens—he was just *beautiful*. Big and proud and magnificently aroused. It should have daunted her; instead it filled her with a sense of longing.

He lowered himself down on top of her, and it felt so wonderfully wicked to feel his hardness pressing against her stomach. 'Weren't you?'

'Yes,' she gasped, forgetting what the question had been.

'And do you know what happens to girls who peep?'

'Yes. No. Yes.'

'This. This is what happens.' But his voice broke just a little, and at the same time as he started to kiss her he thrust into her.

There was only the briefest pain, and she stilled to allow it to pass, looking up to find that he had stilled too, his eyes narrowing in comprehension, and something which looked like his own pain crossed over his face.

But then he began to move again, more gently than before, and she quickly learnt the rhythm, moving in time with him, losing herself in it, chasing it, until she knew that she wanted something more, and he answered her unspoken plea with movements which became faster, harder, driving into her so deeply that she forgot where he began and she ended. And her elusive search was almost over. She had not dreamed it—it surpassed anything she could ever have imagined. She was aware of it sweeping over her for seconds, and then she lost control completely, in a fragment of time which was immeasurable, and as she came slowly back down to earth she heard him moan, saw his eyes close, a look of wild, delirious pleasure on his face, and she shut her own eyes quickly. It seemed almost an intrusion to see him lost in that look of mindless ecstasy.

With Declan still filling her, her head fell sleepily back against the pillow. She felt warm and replete and dazed and satiated. And in love. She nestled luxuriously against him, moving her leg to lie over his leg, loving the intimacy of being able to touch him this way, any way. She did not know what would happen now; she had no experience of after-play. She supposed that they would sleep, wake up and make love again. She hoped.

The last thing in the world she expected was for him to withdraw from her with a swiftness which could have been interpreted as abruptness, and to swing his long, bare legs over the side of the bed.

He walked over to the window, where the moonlight streamed in from a cloud-scudding sky, bathing his sweat-sheened body in milky light. He had his back to her, and when he spoke it was with a tone she had never

heard him use before, and which she couldn't quite
define.

'Why didn't you tell me?'

She knew exactly what he meant. She also knew that
he was angry, and she didn't know why—so she hedged
for time. 'Tell you what?'

It was the wrong thing to say. He turned to face her,
statuesque and magnificent in his nakedness, his face a
series of unreadable, shifting shadows. 'Don't play games
with me, Sam. You know exactly what I mean. Why
didn't you tell me that I was the first?'

Because somehow she had known, even if she had not
acknowledged it at the time, that if she had told him he
would have stopped.

The warm glow which had seeped into her body after
their lovemaking began to ebb rapidly. She tried to keep
the alarm out of her voice. 'Does it matter?'

'Of course it *matters*!'

'Why?' She stared at him in confusion.

He moved closer now, and she searched his face in
vain for a remnant of the softness he had shown during
the act of love. He sighed. 'Because you're—how old?'

She bit her lip. He knew that, surely. He knew from
her c.v. but he had forgotten. 'Twenty-six.'

'Most women of twenty-six . . .' He spoke awkwardly.
'I just assumed——'

'That I wasn't a virgin?' she said bluntly, and saw him
flinch at the word. 'So what? Someone had to be the
first, and——' But she couldn't manage it. The flip retort
lay uneasily on her tongue, and she halted before her
voice cracked.

He sat down on the edge of the bed. Through the window she could see the pale light of dawn stealing the moon's thunder. 'Why not with Bob?'

She shut her eyes briefly. So he wanted to hear about the catalogue of disasters which her love-life had consisted of up until now. And perhaps this, too, was destined to join them. She opened her eyes again. 'Because Bob didn't want me, not in that way. Oh, he put a lot of fancy words to it—told me that he loved me too much, respected me too much not to wait until we were married. And he knew that his mother would disapprove if she found out we were—intimate.' She remembered the sour-faced woman who had wielded such an influence over her only son. 'And she would have found out, undoubtedly. It was a small village; gossip was rife. Which makes it all the more ironic that he should allow my sister to fall straight into his arms, and his bed. But then she's sexy and I'm not!'

He swore softly and grabbed her by the shoulders, levering her up so that she was inches away from him, a light of blinding intensity burning from his eyes. 'Don't even think it,' he commanded. 'There are a lot of men around like your brother-in-law, applying the double standard. This archaic idea that nice girls ''don't''. They turn sex into a bartering weapon. And don't ever compare yourself with your sister, either—she has a superficial gloss that would chip off within the week. Whereas you...' He raised one hand to his mouth, kissed it so gravely that she knew it was the prelude to a farewell. 'You, Sam,' he continued, 'are as sexy as hell.' He saw her disbelieving face. 'Yes! A sensual, giving woman. Which is why...' His voice tailed away for a moment.

'Why it came as such a shock to find that you were a virgin. I'm not in the habit of seducing virgins.'

She was beginning to get angry now. Wasn't it supposed to be the greatest gift you could offer a man? Why, then, did she feel such a fool? 'You mean it's somehow—different?' she finished. She could do little to hide the bitterness in her voice, and she saw his eyes narrow into a hard stare.

'It is different—yes. It's more of a responsibility.'

She shuddered. Responsibility! Now he was making taking her to bed sound like taking out a mortgage! She struggled to sit up, holding the sheet up to cover her breasts. 'I want to go back to my own bed,' she said, lifting her chin firmly, determined that he would see that her pride remained intact.

He put one finger beneath her chin, and gave a half-smile. 'No, you don't,' he contradicted her.

'Yes, I do.'

'You don't——' He bent his head to kiss her softly, touching her breasts as he did so, each one in turn. 'Do you?' he enquired idly, lying down beside her and pulling her down into his arms...

'No,' she said, lost.

She woke up not knowing where she was, to find that he was already awake, propped up on one elbow, surveying her with still watchfulness. Colour washed over her face as memories of the night seeped back: that second time, when he had taken her so quickly, with a swift thoroughness which had left her dazed in his arms. And then, incredibly, again, this time with a sweet slowness, raising her to such a pitch of excitement that she had finally cried out—the waves of satisfaction had gone on and on, dragging at her womb in great powerful sweeps. And then sleep. And now she wished that the night could have gone on like that forever, for she knew no bright hope for the day, not after his shocked re-action to finding that he had been her first lover.

She saw him register her heated colour, but the blue eyes remained as shuttered as ever.

'Hello,' he said softly.

She felt a great wave of relief at the simple greeting. Perhaps things *could* be as perfect as they had been in the night when she'd lain in his arms.

'We need to talk about what's happened, Sam.'

With his words her relief evaporated, and her heart sank. He was going cold-bloodedly to end it, she thought helplessly, and she buried her head in his shoulder, re-fusing to allow him to see her fears. At the touch of her warm cheek on his skin, she felt him start, heard a long sigh escape from his lips.

'Sam?'

'I'm listening.'

'Then look at me.' He pulled her head into his hands, frowning as he observed the suspicious brightness in her eyes. 'The models and the art director will be arriving this morning——'

She stared back at him in bewilderment, as if he had just started speaking to her in another language, and it took seconds for reality to slam its way back into her befuddled brain. All thoughts of work seemed alien. She had forgotten all about their reason for being here—all her thoughts had been for him. But Declan was, nat-urally, the utter professional.

'I don't think it's a good idea if we sleep together while they're here.'

'I see,' she said unhappily. Let's pretend it never happened, was what he was really saying, she concluded.

'No, I don't think you do,' he frowned.

But some illogical demon of jealousy flared up, and the words were out before she could stop them, all her old insecurities giving themselves voice. 'Oh, I think I do, Declan. Have you lined up one of the models for the pleasure of sharing your bed? I'd hate to cramp your style! Just think...' her voice rose with the bitter hysteria inspired by the knowledge that he could dismiss her so lightly '...if you play your cards right you could probably have both of them!'

She flinched at the distaste she saw written on his face, and he moved away from her, getting out of the bed.

'You disappoint me, Sam,' he said, in a cold, quiet voice. 'But I'm not even going to give that the dignity of an answer. Here.' He picked up her discarded satin pyjamas from the floor and dropped them on to the end of the bed. 'You'd better get moving. They're due in a couple of hours.'

And, taking his jeans and a sweater, he walked out of the bedroom without another word, proudly and arrogantly naked, leaving Sam staring after him, knowing that she'd blown it and wanting to curl up and die.

CHAPTER ELEVEN

How could a couple of hours have seemed so long? To Sam, even though she kept herself frantically busy, the wait for the models to arrive seemed the longest of her life.

After Declan had finished in the bathroom, he had reappeared, looking demonically handsome in black jeans and a black polo-neck, the dark tangled hair still damp from the shower. She had been in her own bedroom, her dressing-gown wrapped tightly round her, trying in vain to bring some warmth back into her chilled body, when he had appeared at the door.

'I'm going out, to finalise my backdrops,' he said abruptly. 'I'll be back at eleven.'

The curt way he spoke cut her to the quick, but she raised her chin defiantly. 'Fine,' she replied starkly, then turned away from him, in a gesture of dismissal.

She was aware that he hesitated, and when he finally slammed his way out of the door she knew a feeling that was almost relief, because she didn't have to pretend any more.

I am *not* going to cry, she told herself firmly, as she washed her hair in the bath. I will not give Declan the pleasure of seeing me cry. Although she was someone who had once told him that she wasn't the kind of woman who resorted to tears, she had been doing nothing else ever since.

She looked in the mirror to find that her face was pale and drawn, so she applied a liberal amount of blusher to the high cheekbones, and kohl pencil and plenty of mascara in an attempt to improve the look of her tired and defeated eyes. She finished with lipstick, something she rarely wore, and she scarcely recognised the woman who stared back at her. The lipstick gave definition to her mouth, and the kohl pencil made her feverishly glittering eyes look even bigger than usual.

But it was more than just the make-up. The hint of sadness in the brown eyes, the determined smile which she forced on to her lips—these were directly attributable to Declan Hunt.

It was all so different from how she had imagined it would be. Not the actual lovemaking part—that had surpassed even her wildest dreams. But afterwards. She felt as though someone had given her the moon then snatched it away again.

'I don't think it's a good idea if we sleep together while they're here.' As an innovative way of ending something which had never really begun, Declan should take a prize for that one.

True, she had had no right to accuse him of anything as tacky as wanting to go to bed with the other two models—and his anger had been justified. And yet, she recognised that he had *wanted* to be angry with her, and her hysterical retort had been the excuse he needed to get her out of his bed.

Because Declan had never intended to seduce her. It had been a cruel accident of fate—his nightmare and her comfort mingling in those strange hours of the night where all reality was suspended, to become nothing more than the inevitable reaction of a man to a woman who had shown herself more than willing.

She made herself some black coffee, and, after she'd drunk it, loaded Declan's cameras for him.

Work was the only answer—work as a refuge. Photography was a constant passion, a more reliable love than a man like Declan. A camera couldn't hurt her, couldn't make her feel the way she did right now—so empty and aching inside.

Let Declan imagine that she was about to start pining away for him? Like hell!

He would see that she was made of stronger stuff than that. OK—she had lost her virginity to a man who didn't care tuppence for her, but how many women had that happened to since the beginning of time? She wasn't going to let something like that ruin her life, or her plans. She had thought of nothing but Declan for weeks, and work had come a weak second—and that in itself was madness. For hadn't she worked too hard and too long to throw all her ambitions away on a man who was as out of her reach as a distant planet?

Damn Declan, she thought bitterly. She would show him that she *didn't* care.

And perhaps, in doing that, she might one day be able to convince herself.

A sound at the front door made Sam jump, and with relief she saw that it was the two models and the art directors, unexpectedly early. She was ridiculously pleased to see them, because she had been dreading Declan's return. Defiance in theory was one thing; putting it into practice was another.

The art director was Fraser, an affable Scot who regularly provided Declan with work and whom Sam had met several times in London. 'Hello, Sam,' he said, in his deep burr. 'Have you met Kelly and Jodie?'

Sam put her personal difficulties to one side, and smiled. 'No, I haven't. How do you do? Come in, it's freezing out there.'

Both women topped six feet. Kelly had flaxen ringlets which tumbled down her back, while Jodie provided a stunning brunette version.

'They keep talking about global warming—well, I can't feel any evidence of it down here,' shivered Kelly as she stepped inside.

'It's the wind from the sea,' explained Sam. 'Would you like some coffee?'

'Great idea!' smiled Fraser. He looked around. 'Nice place! Where's the boss?'

'Out getting ideas,' said Sam, as she went out to fill the kettle. Probably about how he can keep me out of his bed at night. Well, he needn't worry. She had thrown herself at him once, and that was once too often. No more.

She made them all coffee and provided a plate of biscuits. Nature, with its usual uneven distribution of gifts, had decided that both Kelly and Jodie should not only have the kind of looks which netted them a small fortune, but had teamed it with the metabolism of teenage boys.

'I can eat *anything*. Literally!' smiled Jodie as another custard cream bit the dust.

'Try some of the logs next to the fire, then,' joked Fraser. He patted his comfortable stomach ruefully. 'This world is far too calorie-obsessed, don't you agree, Sam?'

'Oh, definitely!' she laughed.

He leaned over. 'Here——' And with the tip of his finger he wiped a crumb from the edge of her mouth, looking up as the door slammed shut behind Declan, who walked in, his face thunderous, and stared at Sam.

'What the hell have you done to your face?'

'Declan!' giggled Kelly, the movement causing the flaxen ringlets which snaked down her back to jiggle about. 'Charming as ever, I see!'

For a moment Declan's eyes bored into Sam's, and she stared back at him defiantly. OK, so maybe she *had* overdone the make-up a little, but what did it have to do with him?

Then he seemed to remember that there were three other people in the room, three people, moreover, who were staring at him with open curiosity. 'Kelly. Jodie. Fraser.' He gave a nod at all three, and then smiled, and the effect was devastating. 'Have you seen your rooms yet?'

'We're waiting for the guided tour!' twinkled Jodie.

As they trooped out of the room after him, Sam picked up the tray and carried it out into the kitchen, a burning jealousy licking her from within. And yet she had no right to feel like this—why shouldn't he smile at the models? Jealousy was something she had never been able to understand or to tolerate, and now she was demonstrating the very trait which she so despised in others.

She bent over the sink and started to wash the mugs.

'Sam.' A deep voice came from behind her and she whirled round to see Declan standing there, his blue eyes watchful. 'I didn't mean to startle you.'

Her heart raced and her hands began to tremble so much that she plunged them back into the soapy water to find an imaginary spoon. The smile she gave him was polite, cool and an utter fabrication.

She dropped a spoon back into the soapy water, and gave him a polite smile. 'Are you ready to shoot?'

'Yes.' He frowned. 'No. Not for a minute.' He continued to scrutinise her. 'I don't like all that make-up—it doesn't suit you.'

Unbidden came an image of Gita, gilded with gold and gleaming scarlet. 'Really?' Her tone was icy. 'But that's nothing to do with you, Declan. Is it?' She saw how unexpectedly tense he was; perhaps his deflowered virgin was giving him more trouble than he'd bargained for. She saw the big, strong hands clenched into fists next to the powerful shaft of his thighs. And she remembered how gentle, how persuasive those hands could be, how he had sought and obtained such exquisite response from her during the night with those same hands. Colour washed in flares like war paint over her cheeks and she saw his look, knew that he had guessed what was in her mind.

She had to get out of here. And fast. But he was blocking her way, his closeness both threatening and exciting. 'Now, will you please let me pass?'

He looked down at her in exasperation. 'We need to talk.'

She feigned surprise. 'Oh? I thought we'd said just about everything that needed to be said.'

He swore underneath his breath. 'Don't be so evasive. You know we haven't. And for God's sake will you stop behaving like this?'

'Behaving like what? I'm doing what I thought you wanted—I'm leaving you in peace. You said that you didn't think we should be together while the others were here—well, I'm taking you at your word. Now, will you *please* let me pass? I want to—Declan! What the hell are you——?'

'Shut up!' he bit out savagely, and he caught her by the wrist and pulled her out through the kitchen door, to the back of the house where they couldn't be observed.

He stood towering over her, this big man, and something in his set face sent a *frisson* of fear running down her spine. He was angry with her and she didn't know why.

'What do you want?' she asked in a small voice.

'Shut up,' he said again, and bent his head to kiss her.

It was a kiss that didn't compromise—hard and demanding, as powerful an onslaught as if he had actually made love to her—and she felt her body springing into unwilling response. Helplessly she fell against him as he caught her hips to mould them shamelessly into his own. The power of her body's response to his arousal appalled her. And only when there was no breath left did he end the kiss.

When it was over, he stood looking down at her, his darkly muscular silhouette dominating her horizon.

'What do you want?' was all she could manage.

'At this moment,' he said, with a grim kind of smile, 'I'd like to tear those clothes from your body and bring you to a gasping, weeping climax right here. Because that, my dear, is the kind of effect that you seem to have on me.'

In view of their uneasy confrontation earlier that morning, the words should have shocked her with their blatant statement of physical need untempered by any soft words of love. But they did not shock her; instead they thrilled her, as her imagination conjured up a vivid image to match his words, and she closed her eyes, her cheeks flaring. 'No,' she whispered weakly, but she made no attempt to pull away.

'Oh, yes.' She heard him laugh as he bent his head to whisper in her ear, 'You'd like that, wouldn't you, my sweet, passionate Sam? And so would I. But unfortunately we no longer have the place to ourselves. I don't want an audience when I make love to you again. And I really don't intend to be subjected to an endless stream of innuendo and speculation each morning. I know,' he said grimly, 'just how harmful gossip can be.'

She closed her eyes as an image of Gita swam before her eyes, a constant torment she couldn't dispel.

She made to turn away, but he stopped her.

'The others are leaving tomorrow, as soon as the light fades. We could delay our return by a couple of days. Spend some time here on our own.'

Her eyes searched his face, acknowledging the quickening of her pulse in response to his suggestion. It sounded like heaven, but some self-protective instinct made her fight it.

'What about work, if we stay on?'

'It'll be the weekend,' he reminded her softly. 'What's the matter, Sam—having second thoughts? Regretting what happened last night?'

Was he? Probably.

And was she? Of course she was, knowing that she'd tasted a sweetness with him which could never last. Loving him was a sweet, madness she doubted she would ever recover from.

'And what about our working relationship—now that—this has happened?' she ventured.

He stayed unmoving. 'Now is not the time to make decisions about that. I'm simply asking you to stay for the weekend.'

His words gave her scant comfort. And yet, for now at least, he wanted her. Mousy, inexperienced little Sam. All she had to remember was not to read too much into it. She wondered whether she was asking the impossible in trying to do so, but her lips were already forming the words of acceptance. 'I'll stay,' she whispered.

'Declan!' A voice came from the kitchen, and he dropped his hands from about her waist immediately. The kitchen door swung open, and Kelly came out, wrapped in a pink fun fur, her eyes flicking over the two of them curiously. 'Fraser says to tell you we're ready.'

'Sure.'

It was as though he'd slipped into automatic pilot, thought Sam, as she watched him take charge, and she forced herself to do the same, loading up extra films, his different cameras, she and Fraser lugging most of the equipment along.

They used over half of Declan's locations that first day. The jewellery being modelled was chunky fake, very clever and very expensive, decided Sam as she fingered a string of giant black pearls.

Declan and Fraser had both girls in short black cocktail dresses, laughing and barefooted at the edge of the sea, shoes in hand, their only adornment the jewellery. They looked as if they'd just left an all-night party, and the subliminal message behind the photo was simple, thought Sam—buy this jewellery and you too will have a wonderful time.

He did shots of them sitting on rocks looking out to sea, like Hans Christian Andersen's little mermaid, and more shots on a long-grassed cliff-top, with the wind streaming through their tousled curls.

And, much to Sam's surprise, he let her shoot a roll of film at each of the locations, the first time he had ever done so.

When eventually he straightened up from his camera, the dark head nodded with satisfaction. 'That's it!' he told them.

'Thank God!' sighed Kelly. 'Lead me to the nearest restaurant.'

Back in her bedroom, Sam eyed her selection of clothes with alarm. She hadn't thought to pack anything smart. Not, she thought, as she pulled a simple black sweater over her head, that it was worth trying to compete with the two models.

Easier said than done, for it was difficult not to feel, well, just *ordinary* really, when she saw the other two women dressed to go out for dinner. Both looked amazing in their clinging all-in-ones, with two pelmets masquerading as skirts, showing acres of leg to perfection.

But then she looked up, saw Declan watching her, caught a flash of desire, plain as could be, before the shutters came down over the blue eyes, and she had to turn away on some pretext, a shiver of excitement flickering through her body. He *wants* me, she thought in glorious disbelief. He really does.

Somehow she managed to get through that evening, trying to behave normally, making sure that her face registered nothing of the emotions which were tying her up in knots. But what was 'normal'? She didn't think she knew any more. Was it normal to feel this yearning ache in Declan's company? She wanted to feast her eyes on him, but she couldn't. She wanted to touch him, both possessively and sexually. And there was a full day before she would share his bed with him again.

But that night, as she lay in bed, exhausted after the day, and yet unable to sleep, the door-handle of her room began to turn, and, her heart in her mouth, she stilled to watch Declan move inside and shut the door silently behind him.

Her mouth dried as she saw him, that enticing wrap which he always wore in bed knotted low on his hips.

He didn't say a word as he came to the bed, pulled back the covers and climbed in beside her, taking her into his arms.

'But you said——' she whispered.

'I know what I *said*. And I've changed my mind.'

Just like that. Shouldn't she object to such a cavalier statement? Should she allow him to pick her up and put her down when it suited him? But then he tightened his arms around her, crushing her soft breasts against the muscular, hair-thickened chest, and she felt the slow building-up of heat inside her.

'Declan——'

'Shh,' he whispered. 'Don't say a word. Just kiss me.'

CHAPTER TWELVE

DECLAN left her room as silently as he'd entered, as dawn began to creep in through the window, leaving Sam lying dazed and on the edge of sleep, warm and glowing from the aftermath, recognising the thrill of the illicit in their silent and frantic lovemaking, when he'd kissed her without stopping, his lips silencing her small moans of pleasure.

And the next morning she had to pretend that nothing had happened, hoping that the pinkness in her cheeks and the shine in her eyes looked as if they were due to nothing more than fresh air and exercise. Was she mad, to give herself to him so uninhibitedly?

The day passed with thankful speed, and she watched with envy as Declan became immersed in his camera-work, able to lose himself to the job at hand. And why shouldn't he? He wasn't a lovesick fool, like her.

Oh, she did her own job, but all the time she was constantly aware of him. She consciously had to ration the amount of time she spent surreptitiously admiring every gloriously muscular inch of him, she had to fight to avoid that slanting blue glance, because, in his kind of world, women didn't wear their hearts on their sleeves, and men didn't like adoration, or so all the magazines said. Men liked women who played hard to get.

And so, conversely, even while she longed to be alone with him again, a part of her dreaded it, afraid that he would guess what he meant to her, afraid that her care-

fully maintained façade of just living for the moment
and enjoying what the next few days would bring—which
was presumably what *he* was doing—would quickly
crumble.

So she found herself physically distancing herself after
they'd waved the other three off, rushing around like an
overworked waitress, stacking cups and saucers and
plates.

'I'd better get these washed up,' she babbled as she
saw him approaching her across the room, a slow smile
spreading over his face.

'Did you want to eat in tonight, or——?' Whatever
she had been about to say was swallowed up, and she
realised that she was backing away from him, and when
she reached the wall and could go no further he continued to move towards her, until he reached her, and
rested his arms on the wall above her head, trapping her.

'Hmm?' he queried. 'You were saying?'

'About eating.'

Laughter stirred in the depths of the blue eyes.
'Eating?'

'You're laughing at me,' she accused him.

'No, I'm not. Come here.' He pulled her into his arms.
'Stop looking so scared. What on earth are you scared
about?'

I'll give you three guesses, she thought as she buried
her face in his shoulder. I'm out of my depth here,
Declan. If I can feel this way about you now, then how
can I cope if the feeling intensifies? And once I'm completely hooked, you'll probably leave me...

He pulled her face away from his shoulder and stared
down at her. 'Why don't you go and have a bath, try
and relax, while I cook us some supper?'

That first night he'd just opened tins, and she somehow couldn't reconcile the image of the aggressively masculine Declan was the man who was suggesting stirring things around in pots. 'You can cook?'

'Sure I can. You forget, I've had to fend for myself for a long time.'

Of course he had. He had been a bachelor for thirty-three years. 'Very commendable,' she smiled.

'In fact, I'm probably that elusive man you're searching for,' he drawled. 'I can cook and I can sew— wouldn't you say I'm perfect husband material?'

He was *joking*, for God's sake, but, even so, she didn't trust herself to answer. 'I'll go and run my bath,' she said lightly, wondering what had caused his frown.

But the bath did relax her and she went back into the kitchen to finding him grilling steaks.

'*Very* difficult!' teased Sam.

'Simplicity is the key. Actually I do a mean salmon *en croute*, but the village shop was right out of puff pastry. Here, try this.' He handed her a wooden bowl of mixed salad which he had tossed in a wickedly garlicky dressing. Sam munched a leaf of lamb's-lettuce and sighed.

'Like it?'

'I love it—remind me not to breathe on anyone tomorrow.'

'You can breathe on me,' he said softly.

How could something as innocuous as that start her pulses racing? She put the salad on the table. 'Can I do anything?' she asked shakily.

'You can open some wine. There's a corkscrew over there.'

They ate in the kitchen, but Sam found it difficult to concentrate on anything as mundane as eating. 'So who taught you how to cook?' she asked.

There was a momentary hesitation. 'Gita did, as a matter of fact.'

'Oh?' She hoped that her voice was as bright as the smile which froze her lips. 'Really?'

'Mmm. For a woman who looks as though she's never had to lift a finger in her life she's an excellent cook.'

'Is she?' Sam's reply was so pleasant that it surprised even her, while jealousy lanced through her heart like a javelin. She didn't *want* Gita to be an 'excellent cook', or to have taught Declan. She wanted Gita to be the kind of helpless person who couldn't even boil a kettle.

With an effort, she forced the dark thoughts away.

'So why Gita and not your mother? Didn't she teach you?'

There was a short pause. He had started to look irritated. 'My mother walked out when I was a child—if you must know.'

She saw the heartbreaking bitterness which froze his features for an instant. 'Oh, Declan,' she whispered. 'That's terrible. What happened?'

'I don't talk about it,' he said in clipped tones. 'Would you like cheese?'

She ignored his attempt to change the subject. 'Well, you should,' she said firmly. 'Keeping things bottled up does nobody any good—that's what you told me the other evening.'

'Is it?' he asked wryly. 'Playing the social worker on me now, are you, Sam?'

'I didn't mean to——'

He reached across the table and took her hand. 'I know you didn't. You've just got a soft heart, haven't you? It's not a particularly pretty story.' He turned her hand over and sat staring down at it. 'My parents should never have married. They were totally incompatible. My father was a cold, distant man. My mother, on the other hand, from what I can remember as a small child, was about as different as could be—warm, laughing, giving. I guess she needed more affection than my father was prepared to give her. She thought she'd found it with a much younger man—Laurence, his name was. The only part of the deal that wasn't perfect—for me, anyway—was that Laurence didn't like children. So she left me and my father. But I think she mistook sex for love—a common enough mistake.'

She stared across the table at him, unnerved by those last chilling words. 'What happened?' she whispered.

He shrugged. 'Oh, the man stayed with her until her money had run out, and then she tried to come back. But my father was a proud man, and refused. She came to see me on my tenth birthday with a gift, but he turned her away. There was a scuffle. I remember looking down from my bedroom window, hearing her screaming, the present, still unopened, lying in the gravel by her feet.'

The dark blue eyes imprisoned her. 'It's funny—I haven't thought about that in years.'

Her heart turned. 'Didn't she try to seek custody—or at least *some* access to you?'

'What with? She had no money to employ a lawyer. My father was immensely rich and powerful. I don't think she realised how potentially lethal an adversary he was. I never saw her again. We heard that she died when I was in my early teens. Penniless and alone.'

'Oh, Declan.' Her eyes blinked rapidly. 'That's terrible.'

'Don't cry on me, Sam,' he said gruffly. 'You know what it does to me.' And he pushed away his chair to come round to her, his face set and unreadable as he pulled her up into his arms almost roughly. 'God, I want you,' he said urgently, his words echoing those he'd spoken that first night. 'So badly. Do you know that?'

Yes, she knew—that she, Sam Gilbert, had some inexplicable power over him. Power enough, anyway, to make him desire her with an urgency which seemed to astonish him as much as it did her.

But for how long—and what afterwards? she thought next morning as she cut bread to make sandwiches. How long did such physical infatuation last? Weeks, or months, or simply days? And when it had left him—for she could never imagine it leaving her—how would he end it? Would it take the form of a phone call, or a brief note, an uneasy face-to-face confrontation? She shivered. It was a little like planning your own funeral, she thought. And she assumed that her working relationship with him would only complicate matters...

He came up silently behind her, his arms encircling her waist, pressing his mouth down to the back of her neck, and she closed her eyes helplessly. How could it matter that one day he would leave her when every time it felt this good? Whenever he touched her, she melted.

'Hurry up,' he whispered. 'The day will be over if we don't get out soon. Is that picnic nearly ready?'

She nodded. 'Where are we going?'

'I have somewhere I want to show you.'

'Where's somewhere?'

'Surprise.' He tapped the end of her nose with his finger and smiled, suddenly carefree, and she smiled back, caught up in his mood.

The 'somewhere' proved to be a two-mile walk to a hidden inlet, a small semi-circular beach of gritty white sand, surrounded by charcoal-coloured rocks which were darkly glossy from their recent soaking, for the tide had just begun to retreat. With gulls circling overhead and calling their haunting cry it was lonely and beautiful, and Sam drew in a deep breath of the salty air.

His eyes crinkled. 'Like it?'

'Love it.'

'Let's climb down. Here.' He took her hand and she followed him, scrambling over the rocks to the bottom.

They ate the brown-bread sandwiches with the vast appetites which only fresh air and exercise ever produced, Sam decided, washing them down with cold orange juice, and finishing off with ripe plums from the village shop.

It was so perfect, she thought. Did he manage to enchant *all* his women this way? She looked up to find his eyes on her.

'What is it?' he quizzed.

She swallowed. Well, why not? 'I was wondering if you'd brought lots of others here.' Her voice was deliberately light.

'Others?' He frowned. 'No. I used to come here as a child, after my mother left. Every summer for two weeks—just my father and me—the two of us, alone.'

'And did you have fun?'

'*Fun*?' He sounded surprised, as though fun was not a word you normally associated with childhood, and she supposed that it had been in short supply in his young life.

'It was—OK. He wasn't the kind of man to join in with boyish pursuits. It was a freer world then—and so I used to spend my days exploring. I used to come here and sit for hours, playing in the rock-pools, listening to the sea and the sound of the gulls. It was my secret place.' He gave a sudden, softer grin which knocked years off the hard face. 'Until now. Come here.' And he gathered her close.

There was a crazy fluttering in her heart which his words had produced. He made it sound as though she were the only woman he'd ever brought here, but that must be wrong. He would have brought Gita, surely. And even if he hadn't, then coincidence alone had brought her here today. Because they happened to be down here on a job. Nothing more.

He cupped her face in his hand, staring down at her for a long moment. 'Let's get married,' he said suddenly, and she thought she must have misheard him, because she blinked at him foolishly.

'*What*?' He must be joking, and yet his face was deadly serious.

'Married. Us.'

'*Why*?' It was as though it were happening to someone else, and she stared at him in confusion, aware that her response was not what he had expected, and she wondered how it was possible to want something so badly and yet muck it all up when it actually happened.

He took her hand in between both of his, studying it intently for a moment before looking up again to meet her gaze. 'I can think of all kinds of reasons. We like each other. We make a good team. The physical thing between us is incredible. I respect you, Sam, and respect is a damn good basis for a marriage. You're sweet and kind. I can imagine having children with you.'

She felt slightly sick at this Good Samaritan version of herself. He sounded as if he was reeling off a list of prepared answers to an exam question. And the top answer hadn't even merited a mention—he hadn't said a word about love. But she supposed that there was no reason why he should, for he had never pretended to love her. There had been one great love-affair in Declan's life, the one he'd had with Gita. Cut off and thwarted in its prime. Some men only loved once, and he was obviously one of them.

She knew all this and yet knowing didn't stop the idiotic response she blurted out. 'But most people marry for love, Declan.' She searched his face. Did he have any conception of what she wanted so much to hear him say?

But his answer smashed her foolish dreams.

He brought his dark eyebrows together in a frown. 'Perhaps that's why we have such an appalling record of marriage stability, why so many families break up. My parents married for love, and look at them. Love is a word invented by idealists to sell books and films. What we have, Sam, is a much surer foundation than an emotion which was invented as a polite name for lust.'

So now she knew. He was being honest with her at least, and perhaps she should respect his honesty, respect the fact that he hadn't lied to her, coated his proposal—and what a bizarre and unexpected proposal—with saccharine words of love which meant nothing.

And she realised that there might be another reason for his dramatic proposition. Responsibility. Hadn't he used just that word the other night, when he'd dis-

covered that she was a virgin? Was he simply honouring
that responsibility in a curiously old-fashioned way—by
asking her to marry him?

'I'm not entirely clear as to what kind of marriage
you want, Declan.'

Her cool question seemed to surprise him. 'Meaning?'

'Are you modern enough to want an open marriage?'

His face had become shuttered; the light had died from
his eyes. 'I want exactly the opposite,' he said quietly.
'I want a normal marriage. No infidelity, no mind games.
If we had children, I'd need a commitment that we would
provide a secure home for them to grow up in.'

He wanted, she realised, what he had never had
himself.

He was studying her closely, a glint of light firing
behind narrowed eyes as he noted her hesitation. 'So—
what do you say, Sam?'

He'd never even considered, she thought with a sudden
blaze of anger, that she would refuse him. Oh, no. Declan
was a man who wouldn't underestimate himself.

But the brief flare of anger died almost immediately
because it was all academic anyway, this hesitation of
hers. She loved him too much. She had realised something in the past couple of days, and that was that no
one would ever match Declan in her heart. And if he
hadn't exactly offered her the moon—well, the stars were
near enough.

Imagine, though, if he knew the dark strength of her
feelings for him. She felt as though she could die for
him, would kill for him. She wanted him mind, body,
and soul, with a fierceness which would scare the hell
out of him if he had any idea of its depth. And that

wasn't the kind of relationship he wanted, so it was imperative that she hide it.

She loved him and yes, she would marry him—on his terms, whatever they were—but let him damned well wait for her answer.

It was several seconds before she smiled up at him. 'OK,' she said lightly. 'I'll marry you, Declan. When?'

CHAPTER THIRTEEN

'I DON'T *believe* it!' Michael put his briefcase down beside his desk and stared at her as if she were a Martian.

Sam gave a faint smile, used by now to this astonished reaction—she had encountered it when she'd told her parents and a couple of friends of Declan's that they were getting married.

Michael frowned. 'You're *not*——'

Sam sighed, unable to feel anger with Declan's secretary. At least he had been up-front about it; she'd seen the others peering secretively at her abdomen, searching for a tell-tale swell. 'No, Michael—I'm not pregnant.'

He looked abashed. 'I'm sorry, Sam. I shouldn't have said that. It's just—well, obviously I suspected that Declan was interested in you, and I knew you got on well together. But *marriage*—somehow I——' He went a little pink around the ears, aware that he was digging an even deeper hole for himself. 'Where is he? The prospective groom?'

'Keeping an appointment with an art director. Work goes on, you know.'

'And the wedding? When, where, and, most importantly, am I invited?'

Sam laughed. 'Next weekend, here in London, very small—and yes, of course you are.'

'So soon?'

'Why wait?' she shrugged. Declan did not want to, and neither did she, afraid perhaps that he might come to his senses and call the whole thing off.

'We'd like you to be our witness. Would you, Michael?'

'I'd be honoured,' he answered quietly.

A week left little time to arrange the simple, almost spartan ceremony she wanted. To her astonishment, Declan had suggested a church service, which she had quickly refused. Church weddings were redolent of true romance, love, all the things which most women dreamed of for their wedding-day, and which would be sadly lacking in theirs. No, a church would have been hypocritical.

So they married at Chelsea register office on a bright June morning, with her parents, Charlotte, Bob and Flora as guests, and Michael and John as witnesses. Charlotte looked visibly shocked that her little sister was marrying Declan Hunt.

Sam wore a short-skirted suit of ivory slub silk, and a dramatic wide-brimmed hat in the same ivory. A posy of small, fragrant violets, still dewy damp from the city florist, completed the outfit.

As Michael leaned forward to kiss the cheek of the bride, his face broke into a grin. 'Well done, Sam,' he whispered. 'You must have something that the rest of them didn't.'

That something was her ability to hide how much she loved him, how much each day she grew to depend on him, giving back only as much of herself as she thought he would be able to tolerate, afraid really to let herself go, afraid that if he saw through to how really deeply she was in love with him it would frighten him, make him aware of the gulf between them, of the fundamental inequality of emotion which lay at the heart of their relationship.

The only slight blight on the occasion was the small paragraph in the gossip column of one of the following day's newspapers, which carried an old picture of Declan and *Gita*—with a brief report on the wedding. They obviously didn't have any photos of the bride on file, thought Sam as she gazed resentfully down at the report. She was, after all, a nobody. But what hurt most was Gita's comment: 'I'm very pleased for him, naturally—though obviously a little surprised.'

And what was *that* supposed to mean? thought Sam crossly, before managing to convince herself that it had been sour grapes.

They honeymooned in Paris, where they behaved like shameless tourists, walking every inch of the city, feasting on exquisite food, and making love—with Declan showing a tenderness she found almost unbearably poignant. If only he loved me it would be perfect, she thought. But love was just icing; she must be thankful for the cake.

And she soon discovered that holding back emotionally was a skill which could be learnt, just like baking or riding a horse. Soon, she didn't even realise that she was doing it... And if at times she surprised Declan watching her with a bright, hard stare, then it didn't perturb her. For she was so terrified that he might tire of her—surely he would find emotional distance more intriguing behaviour than being a doormat.

They had been back a week, settling in to a life of working together and living together in Declan's flat. Sam had just finished making a sauce for the pasta while

Declan tossed the salad, when there was a ring at the doorbell, and Sam blinked in surprise when she opened the door.

It was Charlotte.

Sam hardly recognised her sister; she had obviously been out in the rain, because her blonde hair was hanging in bedraggled rats'-tails, the dark roots beginning to show. But her face was pale, her pale blue eyes glittering. She looked strung out.

'Charlotte! What are you doing here?'

Charlotte's eyes flashed over Sam's shoulder to where Declan had started to walk towards the door. 'Is that any kind of greeting to give your sister?' she pouted. 'Aren't you going to invite me in?'

'I'm sorry. Come in, please.'

'Thanks.' Blue saucer eyes flashed. 'Hi, Declan. How's married life?'

He smiled. 'We're surviving, aren't we, Sam?' and put an arm loosely about her shoulder.

Sam grinned happily at her sister; it still thrilled her when he demonstrated his affection like that. It was, she decided, only a little less than perfect.

'Only surviving?' quizzed Charlotte. 'Not much of a superlative for newly-weds. Better try harder, Sam!'

Sam's bubble of happiness burst. 'Here,' she said in a small voice. 'Let me take your coat, Charlotte.' She took the dripping mackintosh. 'Have you had supper?'

'No, I haven't—but I could use a drink first.' Charlotte smiled, tossing her long blonde hair back over her shoulders and sliding herself down on one of the sofas. She tucked her long legs underneath her and looked up at Declan with her amazing eyes.

'What would you like?' he asked.

'A *huge* Scotch, please.'

Declan raised an eyebrow. 'You're pregnant, aren't you?'

Charlotte pouted. 'Oh, Declan—don't be such a bully!'

He turned away. 'Sam?'

Her sister seemed to dominate the room like a bright, shining light, she thought. No matter that Declan had told her, that night he had seduced her, that it was all surface gloss—it was hard to leave years of feeling a very poor second-best behind. 'Just a mineral water.'

He handed out the drinks and Sam looked at Charlotte expectantly, hating the heavy stone of foreboding which lay at the pit of her stomach. 'How long are you staying?' she asked.

Charlotte shrugged. 'How long can you put up with me? Oh, you might as well know—I've left Bob!' she announced dramatically.

Sam swallowed. She saw Declan's mouth twist into a derisory line. 'Where's Flora?' she asked immediately.

'With Mother—they've said they'll have her for a few days while I—have a little space for myself.'

Sam thought how trite she sounded. 'But what about the baby?'

Charlotte's mouth tightened. 'I'm not even thinking about the baby at the moment.'

'Is there any chance you'll be able to work things out between you?' Declan sipped his drink and stared over the rim of his glass at Charlotte.

'Who knows?' She gave him a sideways glance. 'I think he's still carrying a torch for Sam, you know.'

Sam went pink, saw Declan's swift stare, and grew even more confused. 'I—I'm sure you're wrong.'

The saucer-like eyes became amused. 'I'm not wrong, Sam. Such a pity we decided all this *after* the marriage, isn't it?' She gave a high, tinkling laugh.

Sam was too stung by Declan's black expression to do little more than stand up and say to Charlotte, 'Have you luggage?'

'It's in the car—but don't worry about me—I can sleep on the sofa.'

'That won't be necessary,' said Declan, in a cold voice. 'You can use one of the guest rooms.'

Over supper, Charlotte drank more wine than she should have done and flirted outrageously with Declan all evening, and Sam just sat and observed. It was like watching a horror film, she thought: you were repelled and yet unable to tear your eyes away. Eventually, Charlotte stretched and yawned, the movement emphasising her small, neat breasts.

'Bed for me,' she said sleepily. 'Or would you like me to help you clear up?'

'I'll do it,' said Sam.

'*We'll* do it,' amended Declan.

'No. You go and bring Charlotte's luggage up from the car,' replied Sam stiffly. She was going to confront her fears. If she showed Charlotte that she didn't mind her being alone with Declan, it would also show her that she was not afraid of her.

But she burnt her hand washing out a saucepan as she heard them come laughing up the stairs together, and, after she'd loaded up the dishwasher, went into their bathroom, taking far longer under the shower than usual, so that Declan was almost asleep when she climbed into bed and he pulled her against his naked body.

'Why on earth did you ask your sister to stay?' he grumbled, his hand stroking the small of her back.

She felt tired and headachy after having to endure the long evening. 'I could hardly have turned her out on to the street,' she snapped. 'Could I?'

'There are such things as hotels.'

'Oh, for goodness' sake,' she said crossly. 'She's family. And anyway, I noticed that the two of you seemed to be enjoying some private joke on the stairs.' They were having a row, she realised. Their first row. Over Charlotte.

'I was playing the dutiful brother-in-law,' he whispered into her ear, and slid his thigh in between hers.

But she thought of Charlotte in the next room, perhaps listening, beautiful and lithe, her blonde hair spread all over the pillow, and she knew that tonight she just couldn't. 'Please, don't, Declan,' she said quietly. 'I'm tired.'

He withdrew his leg immediately. 'Goodnight,' he said, and gave her a perfunctory kiss on the end of her nose, but there was an unmistakable note of irritation in his voice, far more than just a refusal to make love warranted, so that it came as no surprise when he turned over instead of taking her in his arms as he usually did. He was asleep within seconds.

While she lay miserably awake for hours.

It was the first time that they'd gone to bed together and not made love, and she felt completely empty inside, as if someone had turned a blow-torch on her, and wiped away all her feelings. Not just because she wasn't slipping into sleep in that delicious post-lovemaking daze with Declan clutching her firmly to him. It went deeper than that, and it matched the foreboding she'd felt since

Charlotte had first rung the doorbell: that tonight something had died between them.

Charlotte stayed for four days, spending every mealtime with them, dominating the conversation, as was her wont, with her inconsequential chatter about this and that, seemingly oblivious to the charged atmosphere.

On the morning of the fourth day, Declan and Sam were alone in the studio, when he turned to her. 'I want your sister out of our home.'

She knew that Charlotte flirted with Declan. Perhaps he's afraid he'll succumb, she thought masochistically as she loaded up his camera for him.

He gripped her arms so tightly that she almost dropped the camera. 'Are you listening to me, Sam? I said get rid of her!'

'How?'

'It's easy,' he said, between gritted teeth. 'You go upstairs, you tell her we're only just married, and we want to be on our own.' His eyes blazed. 'Do you realise that we haven't made love in all the time she's been with us?'

She flinched from the accusation he'd justifiably levelled at her. 'She might hear,' she said lamely.

'But you didn't care about that when we were in Sussex, did you? My God—you were different then— you'd hardly let me leave your bed that night, would you?'

The colour drained from her face as she acknowledged the bitterness in his voice. That was then, she thought desperately, and this is now, and something's happening to us. She nodded. 'All right, I'll go up and tell her today.'

'Good!'

'I'll tell her at lunchtime.' In her distracted state she hadn't had a chance to look in the diary. She eyed him in the pale grey linen suit he wore, one of several he used for business meetings at the various advertising agencies. 'You're going out later, are you?'

'Yes,' he got out, and slammed out of the studio into the office.

She had never known him quite so bad-tempered, even in the early days of working for him. Was that because he was sexually frustrated? Or did he genuinely not like having Charlotte around?

But one part of Sam was petrified. What if things were no better between them when Charlotte left? What if the cloud which seemed to be blighting their relationship did not lift?

The studio shoot went reasonably well, although Declan was terse with her all morning, and after he'd left for his lunch she climbed the wrought-iron steps up to the apartment with reluctant feet.

She halted as she opened the door, startled to hear the incongruously sultry throb of a saxophone as it wafted through the sitting-room. The front door slammed behind her, and Charlotte came out of her bedroom, wearing nothing but her underwear.

'Oh, it's you,' she said, and had the grace to look momentarily abashed.

'Yes,' said Sam, feeling sick. 'Who did you think it would be—Declan?'

Charlotte's hair was newly washed and brushed, a flaxen curtain that made Sam think of Heidi, except that the eyes were made up like those of a nightclub singer. She was wearing nothing but black silk panties which were little more than a brief V shape over her tanned hips, and a matching bra, cunningly cut so that her tiny breasts were pulled together to give a small and magnificent cleavage. There was barely a curve to her belly to give any hint of her condition.

Sam was honestly afraid that she might be sick all over the floor. 'Who did you think it would be?' she repeated in a gasping whisper. 'Declan?'

Charlotte shrugged, her eyes defiant. 'Why not? You must have realised that he isn't immune to me?'

No, indeed. He'd said as much that morning when he'd told Sam to get rid of her. 'Because he's my—husband,' she stammered out weakly. 'Doesn't that matter to you?'

Years of hatred came spilling out of Charlotte's mouth. 'What matters to me is that I see a man who is *wasted* on you—utterly wasted. Sam, with her sickeningly sweet smile, her butter-wouldn't-melt expression. Did he fall for it? But, by God, he's regretting it now, isn't he? It's written all over his face. I can see it every time he looks at me, every time he watches me moving around. He wants me, Sam—the way all your men have always wanted me!'

'I don't believe you,' said Sam in a quiet, shocked voice. 'You've always been greedy, Charlotte—you've always had more than enough for yourself—toys, friends, men. But it wasn't enough for you—you wanted more. You had to have mine, too. Well, you shan't have Declan because he's seen through you, because he's mine and because I love him. So get your stuff and get out, before I—before I...' Her voice tailed off. You couldn't, after all, physically threaten a pregnant woman.

Charlotte's face had whitened, but she stood her ground, a familiar knowing smile on her mouth which

frightened Sam. 'You little *fool*,' she said, her face con-
torted with scorn. 'You really have no idea, do you?
What he's like? All right, I admit, I thought that Declan
was fair game—men who play around usually are.'

Sam's knees trembled with fear. 'What are you talking
about?'

'He's still seeing the other one, isn't he—the model—
what's her name? Gita. That's it. And I just thought
that he might like something in the way of a change.'

Sam swallowed. Gita. 'You're lying, Charlotte. I don't
believe you—you're lying. That was all over years ago.'

'But he really loved her, didn't he? Everyone in the
business knew that. He was heartbroken when she
became Lady Squires—that's why he stayed in America
all that time—he couldn't face coming back and seeing
them together.'

Sam fought for strength. 'That's history, Charlotte.'

'Is it?' asked Charlotte in an ominously quiet voice.
'Then why has she rung him here?'

'I don't believe you.'

'You'd better.' She gave a malicious smile. 'Where do
you think your precious Declan is today?'

'He's gone out to lunch.'

'With *her*!'

'No.' It was a small whisper, like a dog who'd been
beaten. 'With a client.'

'You don't believe me? Well, try this for size. I overheard him arranging to meet her. One o'clock at the
Savoy. Prove me wrong, Sam—check it out.'

Like a mechanical figure, Sam looked at the watch on
her wrist and had trouble focusing her eyes. The dial
seemed an awfully long way away. It said twelve-thirty.

Time enough. Forgetting Charlotte, moving stiffly like a shock victim, she opened the door and walked out.

The July sales were in full blast, eager tourists bustling in and out of the shops on the Strand. And just off it, in an inconspicuous little courtyard, lay one of London's most famous hotels, the habitual line of black cabs outside being orchestrated by a liveried doorman.

No one stopped her as she went in. She had heard that unaccompanied women were viewed by hotels with suspicion, but a wry smile twisted her mouth. Ladies of the oldest profession were unlikely to have small, scrubbed pale faces with big frightened eyes. Or be wearing white jeans and a white silk shirt which drained her face still further.

She walked through the circular foyer, through the luxuriously carpeted section where people sat sipping drinks and eating from bowls of up-market nibbles. A man approached her.

'Madam is looking for someone?'

She shook her head, then changed her mind, and nodded. 'Please. Just a peep. It's a—surprise.' She knew she sounded young, gauche even, and she was unprepared for his gentle smile and nod.

'Certainly, madam.'

The restaurant area was big enough, crowded enough and full of enough muted conversation for her to stand unnoticed on the sidelines and scan the room.

But she didn't have to stand there for long. She spotted them at once—they were far too striking a couple to be missed by anyone.

Gita wore scarlet; she looked like a poppy, her hair caught into a dramatic topknot of gleaming ebony.

Declan, with dark curls to rival Gita's, sat with his head slightly to one side, smiling at something she said.

As she watched, Gita placed one beautifully manicured hand over Declan's and then laced her fingers intimately with his. Then she leant forward, whispered something in his ear, and slowly and very softly pressed her lips against his cheek.

He didn't resist, he let them lie there, and, with a choked sound in the back of her throat, Sam fled.

She was aware of the startled faces which turned in her direction as she made her way out of the hotel, gulping in great breaths of air when she got outside, but still not wanting to stop, wanting to put as much distance in between herself and the place where her husband was cavorting with his lover, as though their very proximity might itself contaminate her.

She was in a taxi straight away, propelled inside by the doorman, who looked at her anxiously, as if she needed to be taken to the nearest hospital.

'Are you all right, miss?'

She nodded as he shut the cab door. All right? No, she was not all right. She could never imagine feeling all right again in her life.

She directed the taxi back to the studio instinctively, then made it stop two streets away. She couldn't go back there. She couldn't. That place was not her home any more.

She wandered the streets sightlessly, oblivious to the concerned looks of the passers-by, a horrible fear taking root in her mind and growing by the second.

Had she been the most gullible fool in the world? Had Declan's wooing of her all been part of a sophisticated plan? What if he'd been seeing Gita since he arrived back in England, but Robin was growing suspicious? What if Gita had refused to leave Robin, and relinquish her title, but had agreed to continue the affair? Everyone had seen the sparks which flew between them that night at the awards, Robin included—Sam remembered his tight-lipped expression.

So what would ensure that no suspicions would alight on them, and make Robin suspect that the affair was continuing?

If Declan were *married*.

Because no one would be cynical enough to believe that Declan would cheat on a new bride he was madly in love with.

A sob, long suppressed, rose in her throat and came out in a slow, choking noise.

But he wasn't in love with her; he'd as good as told her that. He saw in her the faithful little Samaritan he *respected*—God, how she hated that word—whom he could rely on to provide him with a secure base, both at home and at work.

Sanity fought to contradict her, but she was no longer sane, and, without knowing that she'd done so, she turned blindly into the road, totally unaware of the large black London cab, until she heard the desperate screech of the brakes as the driver attempted, and failed, to miss her.

CHAPTER FOURTEEN

SAM slowly opened her eyes to become aware of two things: that she was lying in a hospital bed with Declan at her side, and that her head throbbed alarmingly. She tried to sit up, and found to her astonishment that it needed more effort than she was prepared to make.

She stared into blue eyes which looked so unusually sombre that she instinctively attempted to lift a hand with which to comfort him, when memory returned, and with it pain, and she tried to sit up again, but it hurt too much.

'What——?' she croaked, but her lips were dry, and he shook his head.

'Shh. Don't say anything.' And then she heard him calling with a kind of desperation for the nurse.

They wouldn't allow her to have the cool water her parched throat cried out for until a doctor appeared, and the curtains were drawn, and they were asking Declan to leave, but she heard his savage refusal. Lights were being shone in her eyes, her knees and ankles being hit with pieces of metal, the sole of her foot scratched with a pin. It was all too intrusive. She gave a whimper of pain, and Declan swore.

'Can't you stop the pain for her?' he demanded savagely.

She heard low, conciliatory words, and the nurse was pressing a small plastic container to her mouth. The thick liquid was bitter and she screwed her nose up, but she drank it anyway, and quite quickly, it seemed, she allowed sleep to carry her off to where there was no pain, no memory.

He took her home. That was, he took her to his flat; she had stopped thinking of it as home that day at the hotel. She didn't want to go, but what choice did she have? She couldn't go to her parents, couldn't face seeing Charlotte's knowing smile. And she couldn't go home to her own flat because the doctor had adamantly forbidden her to be discharged unless there was someone to look after her.

'Head injury can be idiosyncratic,' he had warned darkly, which Sam took to mean that she could pass out again without warning. So, for the next few days at least, she was reliant on the man who had not only destroyed her trust but her life, too.

He had cancelled three jobs, he told her, in that oddly formal voice he had used all the time she'd been in hospital, and asked the clients if they would like to use someone else, but they had preferred to wait. She had been knocked out by the taxi, but that was all.

She sat very still in bed, as, white-faced, he stared at her. 'In God's name, Sam—what got into you? The taxi driver said you just rushed straight out in front of him.'

She stared at him for a long moment, so tempted to bite out an accusation, yet so flabbergasted by the duplicity demonstrated in his astonishment that she was rendered speechless, before she realised that unless Charlotte had said something—which she doubted— Declan would have no idea that she knew about him and Gita. And the less she remembered about that day, the better. She shook her head tiredly. 'I don't want to talk about it. Or think about it.'

He frowned. 'You're lucky you weren't killed.'

Lucky? She didn't feel in the slightest bit lucky, she thought, as he pulled the duvet over her with hands which had not attempted in any way to touch her. Had they touched Gita, while she'd been in hospital? she wondered, with bitter pain. Touched her with the same tenderness she had witnessed in Gita's kiss?

She turned her head into the pillow, unable to speak of it, or even to think of it, because the memory of it was searing her like a naked flame held to her flesh.

Declan prowled around the flat like a caged tiger. He was silent, and so was she; they had nothing left to say to one another. She often found him watching her covertly, his eyes narrowing when he met her blank stare.

She waited, like a chick nesting her young, for her body to mend, knowing that she was simply putting off the inevitable.

Within three days, her body, if not her mind, had recovered. They sat together in the sitting-room drinking tea, with golden sunshine like liquid honey bathing the room in light. Taking a deep breath, Sam put her cup and saucer carefully down on the table.

'We have to get a divorce,' she said quietly, without preamble.

Their eyes met in a long silence.

'If that's what you want.'

And how that hurt. She had known that would be his response, had expected it—but hadn't there been one last forlorn hope inside her that had prayed for his protestation? Some idiotic belief that she had dreamt the whole incident? She closed her eyes.

'It was a mistake,' he said. 'A mistake to expect——'

'No!' Her eyelids fluttered open as she interrupted him. 'Please, Declan, don't say any more. Not another word. Please. Let's not hurt one another. Let's just call it a day. Let's end it in a civilised way.'

His mouth twisted into an ugly line. '*Civilised*?' His voice was harsh and incredulous, and he turned to look out of the window, his hands deep in the pockets of his faded denims, and when he turned back his brief flare of temper appeared to be forgotten. 'Very well, Sam,' he said coolly. 'We'll be civilised. How do you suggest we go about it?'

Within the week she was out of his life. She moved back into her old flat and quickly managed to find herself another job as an assistant.

She soon found out why she was able to fill the post at such short notice and why the last assistant hadn't stopped to work out their notice—it was frightful.

The work was as limiting as a strait-jacket. The studio specialised mainly in passport photos and ghastly portraits of spoilt children who threw tantrums, who even Sam—who loved children—couldn't get through to, mainly because she was incarcerated in the dark-room nearly all day.

So unlike working for Declan, came the unbidden thought before she firmly put it out of her mind. It had been her mid-week resolution—that all thoughts of Declan Hunt were strictly forbidden.

She had started setting herself targets—how long could she go without thinking about him? After the first week she had managed to work up to a whole hour, but the days were hard to get through—pretending that she was fine, instead of breaking up inside—and it was a relief to get home, to shut the door and allow herself the luxury of tears.

She started buying magazines, since they seemed to give out a lot of advice she could use. One of them had

been very helpful—'How to Handle Life without Him'.
The most important thing, apparently, was to give
yourself a change of image, so she'd started growing her
hair. This was also a good thing since 'the most beautiful
gift a woman can give to a man is her long hair'. So that
was where she'd been going wrong all these years.

But she felt she was fighting a losing battle in the
glamour stakes—she'd lost so much weight that most of
her clothes swam on her, and her brown eyes looked
huge in a pale, pinched face.

Busy was better, she decided. Work filled up some of
the gaping emptiness in her life, but weekends were in-
tolerable. Since Declan's exposé on the youth club, not
only donations but offers of help had flooded in. The
club had been besieged with people all much younger
and more dynamic than Sam, including another social
worker, Lucy, who was now heavily involved with John.

'Take a few weeks away, Sam,' John had smiled.
'You've only just got married, after all. *Enjoy!*'

'I'm sure she'll enjoy all that money,' Lucy had put
in rather wistfully.

Because she hadn't dared tell anyone yet that her marriage was over. It was still too raw, too humiliating. She
imagined that Declan would serve her divorce papers
soon enough, and she couldn't have cared less when that
was—next week or never. She knew that she would never
want to marry anyone else.

And then, one Saturday morning, the day yawning
ahead of her, she was flicking through her magazine
when she saw it.

It was a photo of Kelly and Jodie for the jewellery
campaign, taken on location in Sussex. She stared at the
glossy double spread in amazement.

Declan had used *her* photograph.

She was restless all week after seeing it. It was a good photo—the kind that she was no longer taking, trapped in this hell-hole of a studio. On the morning her boss asked her to chat the rep up to try to get a reduced price on black and white films, something inside her snapped.

I'm going to chuck it all in, she thought recklessly. Go and work the summer abroad and forget all about that conniving snake Declan Hunt.

An agency promised her work as an au pair in Marseilles. 'Though you are a little *old*,' the woman said doubtfully. 'Bring your passport in tomorrow morning. We're open until twelve on Saturdays.'

The only problem was that Declan had tucked her passport away with his after their honeymoon. She'd been in such a rush to get away from him that she'd hurriedly flung all her belongings together and forgotten *that*.

She had cycled to within a street of his studio when her nerve almost failed her, and she would have turned back had her excuse to see him not been such a legitimate one. Why hadn't he sent the wretched thing on? Then, at least, she would have been denied the heart-breaking necessity of seeing him again.

She rang the doorbell, although as she did it occurred to her that she could have used her own key—he had never asked for it back.

He took so long to answer it that she was on the point of turning away when he appeared, and she stared at him, speechless with shock.

He looked dreadful: gaunt, his jaw as heavily shadowed as his eyes. He was dressed from head to toe in black denim, and this only emphasised his strange grey pallor. The thick, tangled black curls were more unruly than ever.

Her heart turned over with love and pain. Her instinctively protective question escaped before she could stop it. 'What's wrong with you, Declan? Are you ill?'

His mouth twisted into a grim parody of a smile. 'No, Sam—I'm fine; never better. How about you?'

'I'm fine, too.'

'You'd better come in.'

She entered the flat nervously, glancing around her with dread, half expecting to see some evidence of Gita's occupancy, but there was none, and she hadn't even realised that she had been holding her breath until a long sigh escaped from her lips.

Abruptly, he strode over to where the drinks were kept. 'Do you want a drink?'

Was this the same Declan? The man who never drank during the day? 'It's only just past twelve,' she pointed out.

'When I need someone to help me tell the time, I'll ask,' he grated, and poured himself a brandy. He looked at her over the rim of his glass, blue eyes narrowed in observation. 'Don't lose any more weight, Sam. I know thin is in, but that half-starved look is particularly unattractive.'

She felt bewildered by the insult. 'I didn't come here to be insulted.'

'Oh? Just what did you come here for? What do you want?'

She hadn't expected such aggression, and it filled her with anger. *He* was the one who had reneged on the deal by continuing to see Gita. And he had admitted himself that the marriage had been a 'mistake'. And yet here she was, compliantly giving him a separation without acrimony, so he certainly had no right to be angry with her.

She shook her head in defeat. 'I've come for my passport.'

'Your passport?' he answered sharply. 'You're going abroad?'

She stared at him. What did he care? 'Obviously.'

He scowled. 'Wait there.'

It was painful to watch him walk into what had once been *their* bedroom, and she had to steel the tears not to well up in her eyes.

He was back in a moment with her passport, and as he handed it to her there was the briefest contact. Involuntarily she shivered. It's still there, she thought helplessly. Nothing has changed since the day I first came here for the job, except that now it's a million times stronger, a million times worse.

'Who are you going with?'

She resented his question, and his tone, and lifted her chin. 'That's really none of your business.'

'No.' He gave a heavy sigh. 'You're right.' Then he raised his eyebrows in arrogant query. 'Will there be anything else?'

She would *not* be dismissed like a servant! 'Actually, yes.'

'There is?' He spun round to stare down into her eyes.

'I'd like to know why you used my picture in the "Gem" campaign?'

He gave a short, humourless laugh. 'I should have guessed,' he said bitterly. 'Work.'

She looked at him questioningly. 'Why?'

He shrugged broad shoulders. 'Because it was the best.'

She stared at him in disbelief. 'Better than yours?'

His mouth made a disparaging line. 'Yes. So there you have it, Sam—my professional endorsement of your ability as a photographer. You should go far. And now——' he looked at his watch, and then back to her dismissively '—if that is all—I have work to do.'

On Saturday? There's no need to lie, Declan, she thought sadly. I'm going anyway. And this time she knew that nothing would bring her back.

She turned to go when her eye was caught by a black and white photo lying casually on the table.

It showed a youth of around seventeen, a blanket wrapped around him, sitting on the steps of an imposingly grand theatre, his hand held out for spare coins. It was a stark and powerful representation of urban decay.

She picked it up. 'Where was this taken?'

'Here,' he said shortly. 'In London.'

'What's it for?'

He sighed. 'I've decided to go back into photo journalism. You see, you were right all along, Sam—my forte *does* lie in social documentation. My heart isn't in the other stuff any more. I knew that when I compared your photos with mine.'

'Oh.' She was dumbfounded, and yet strangely satisfied. Had she influenced him at all, even a little? But then memory intruded, and, shamefully, spite.

'So you're closing down your studio?'

'I'm thinking about it. I'll probably rent it out to start with and I'll keep my dark-room facilities, naturally. But I won't be doing studio shoots any more.'

She gave him a brittle smile. 'Oh, dear—what will Gita say?'

He didn't speak, but looked at her as if she'd just invented a new word. 'What did you say?' he asked quietly.

She swallowed, trying to quash the jealousy and the anger, but to no avail. 'Gita. She likes the good life, doesn't she? Photo journalism won't be quite so lucrative, will it? Or was she planning to carry on living with Robin while she sees you?'

He took a step forward then, his eyes almost black with anger. 'You'd better explain what you just said,' he said, his voice dangerously soft.

How *dared* he play the wounded one? 'It's all right, Declan—I *know*!'

'Know?'

'About you and Gita.'

He studied her dispassionately before he spoke. 'I think you'd better tell me, don't you, just what you're talking about?'

'I *saw* you—with Gita—at the Savoy. She was...' Her voice shook. 'Was—kissing you.'

He remained implacable. 'I see. You, of course, just *happened* to be at the Savoy.'

She turned on him. 'Don't you *dare* criticise me! You're the one who wanted a faithful marriage and you're the one who reneged on that. All that stuff about secure bases for families to grow was just so much tosh!'

'So how did you trace me to the Savoy?' he asked.

'Charlotte told me! She overheard you. She—oh, my God, she——' And she started sobbing.

He didn't hold her as he once would have held her; instead he gently sat her down on the sofa, as he would someone who was very sick. And she was. Lovesick.

'Tell me about it,' he suggested.

'I don't want to tell you about it!' she wailed. 'I want a handkerchief.'

'Here.'

She buried her nose in the white linen, then wished she hadn't, because his own unique, heavenly masculine smell had permeated even that. 'There's no point in raking all this up,' she said, once her equilibrium had returned.

'I disagree. I want to hear everything. Starting with Charlotte.'

She glared at him, the anger and the bitter heartbreak she'd suppressed for weeks finally boiling over. 'All right, I will! That morning you told me she had to go—I came up here.' She stared at him accusingly. 'She was in her bra and pants! Almost naked! Waiting for you!'

He nodded. 'And?'

'*And*?' she almost screamed at him. 'Is that all you can say?'

'What do you expect me to say?' he answered coolly. 'That it comes as a shock? Then I'd be lying. What did she say?'

'She told me that you had been watching her, desiring her—— '

His mouth was a grim line. 'And you believed her—naturally?'

She looked at him wide-eyed, hearing the bitterness in his accusation. 'Well, no—I didn't, actually. I told her that it was all in her imagination.' For a second the hard, cold eyes were lit by the burning gaze she knew so well, but only for a second. He lounged back in the sofa, his arms behind his head, watching her.

'I suspected that sooner or later she would come to the point in her own over-the-top way,' he remarked. 'Which is precisely why I told you to get rid of her. So what happened next?'

'She told me that I was naïve about men, that I always had been. She said that everyone knew how much you'd been in love with Gita, and that she'd overheard you arranging to meet.'

'Which was when, presumably, you came dashing over to the Savoy?'

She nodded. 'So now you know,' she said bitterly.

'No, sweetheart,' he answered savagely, managing to make the endearment sound like an insult. 'I don't know, and neither do you.'

She made to get up. 'I don't want——'

'Shut up,' he said, ruthlessly, and pulled her back down beside him. 'Before you go, you will *listen*, only this time you're going to get the correct version of my relationship with Gita, from start to finish. No lies, no gossip—the plain, unvarnished truth.'

'I don't want to hear,' she whispered.

He lifted a hand to silence her. 'Whether you *want* to or not is not up for discussion, Sam. You are going to hear, like it or not. You owe me that much.' The blue eyes gave off angry little sparks. A muscle worked furiously in one tense cheek.

'After I'd worked as Robin's assistant I set up my own studio using some of my inheritance, and Gita came to work for me as *my* assistant.' He sighed. 'She was very young, very beautiful, and yes, we *did* have a relationship—but it was never more than a very pleasant interlude—at least on my part. I was never in love with her.'

'But everyone says——'

'I know what everyone *says*,' he interrupted impatiently. 'And I'm telling you it isn't true.' He stared at her and shook his head slightly. 'Listen. Gita had a fragile ego. Just *who* ended the relationship meant a great deal to her, but nothing to me, and so I went along with her telling everyone that she had grown tired of me, and had fallen in love with Robin.'

'But she hadn't, had she?' said Sam suddenly. 'Fallen in love with Robin, that is. She *was* in love with you, wasn't she?'

'Yes,' he said quietly. 'That's why I went to work in the States when I finished my war photography. I left it for a decent enough interval so that when I came back—and I had always intended to come back—she would have got over me. But she hadn't. Over the years she had convinced herself that what we had once shared was the modern-day equivalent of Romeo and Juliet. Soon after I returned she began to phone me, send photos of herself. But it was after she kept giving interviews about me that I knew it had to stop. For her sake, and for Robin's. So I met her once, alone, to tell her as much. That I was never going to be interested in her again, because——' He hesitated, then seemed to change his mind. 'And that she should give her marriage a last try.'

He gave a wry smile. 'Ironically, when she asked me to meet her at the Savoy, it was to thank me for making her see sense—to tell me that things were better between her and Robin, and that she was pregnant at last, after years of believing they would never be able to have a child.

'And so, you see, your whole Gita saga was nothing more than a series of misunderstandings; convenient, perhaps—for you, Sam.'

She stared up at him. 'Convenient? For me? What are you talking about?'

'Because they gave you a legitimate excuse for ending our marriage, didn't they? Instead of asking me, you chose to run away. But it wasn't just a physical withdrawal, was it? Because I sensed your mental withdrawal before that. It started in Paris, but when did it *really* happen? When was it, Sam? When Charlotte brought the news that she and Bob had finally split up, *were* you thinking that it had come just weeks too late? That now you were married to me, when it should have been him?'

She shook her head in disbelief. 'You can't honestly think that I preferred Bob to you.'

'Can't I? You continued to see him, even after he was married. I saw him waiting to take you out to dinner, remember?'

'He wanted to talk to me about the state of his marriage,' she protested.

'How convenient,' he said coldly. 'So how was it that after years of remaining celibate you chose to give yourself to me after you'd spent the afternoon with your family, and Bob? What was it, Sam—did it finally get too much? Did the sight of him make you hot for someone—anyone?' His voice had lowered to an insulting drawl. 'I thought at the time that you were using me as a substitute, and maybe I was right. Tell me, did you close your eyes and think it was him?'

'Stop it!' she yelled. 'That isn't true, and you damn well know it, Declan!'

'Why me, then?' he asked quietly. 'Why no one else?'

'Because every man I ever met used to repulse me; I'd go out with them once and they'd try to make love to me and——'

'But *I* did that,' he pointed out. 'So why me?'

'Just because——' Her voice faltered; she couldn't say it. 'Because it was you.'

'So if you felt enough for me to let me be the man to give yourself to, the man you agreed to marry, then what happened after the wedding, Sam? What happened to the sparky, feisty, tender woman I married? Oh, she was there, sometimes, usually in bed, but for the rest of the time she retreated so that I could no longer reach her. What happened, Sam—to make you become untouchable? A cardboard cut-out of the woman I knew and...' He shook his head, almost in defeat, as if he'd said enough. 'I'd just like to know what happened to make you like that.'

The bitter way he spoke made it clear that he had little or no regard left for her, and that broke her heart. She had been stupidly wrong about Gita, but Declan was right—the real reason why things had not worked out was that she had felt too much, while he had not felt enough.

She looked up at him. Would the truth redeem her, so that perhaps whenever he remembered her, if he remembered her, it might be with something resembling the affection he'd once felt?

'You did,' she answered quietly. 'You made me distant. Or, rather, my insecurity about you did.'

He had gone very still, like a cold black statue. 'Explain,' he shot out.

Was it shameful to admit how much she loved him? 'I loved you, "not wisely but too well".' She tried to make the quote sound light-hearted, but the crack in her voice betrayed her.

'What are you talking about?'

'I loved you so much that it frightened me. It overwhelmed me—and I knew that you could never feel that way about me. You'd told me so yourself, that love was a word you didn't believe in. I sort of thought that it might *trouble* you to know just how dependent I was on you. And so I used to pretend.'

'Pretend?'

She nodded. 'Pretend that I felt the same way as you
did. You know, compatibility combined with the physical
thing——'

'Did I ever really say that?' He sounded disgusted.

She had given too much away, but now that she had
started she couldn't seem to stop. 'I was afraid that once
I opened the floodgates that would be it—that the
strength of my love would frighten you out of my life.'

'And so you locked a part of yourself away from me,
and I couldn't reach you,' he said, half to himself, and
he dropped to his knees on the floor in front of her and
lifted both her small, cold hands into his. 'I couldn't
reach you because I didn't have the courage to tell you
what I had discovered about myself.'

She stared at him in bewilderment.

'That I was fathoms deep in love with you,' he concluded softly.

She shook her head distractedly. He was just saying
it. 'No.'

He gave a sad smile. 'You see, you don't believe me
now—you wouldn't have believed me then, would you?
And why should you have done—after all I'd said?'

And she stared at him, knowing that he was right.
That, after what he had said about love, her insecurity
about herself and their relationship would have made it
impossible for her to believe that he meant it.

'But that day, when I asked for the divorce—you said
that it had been a mistake——'

'A mistake to think that you could ever love me as
much as I had come to love you. You didn't even want
to discuss it, and I thought you'd simply had enough.'

And just as she had spoken the truth to him at last,
she now recognised the truth which sprang from his lips.
Her mouth began to tremble as she stared at him.

'*I love you*, Sam,' he whispered. 'I think I always have done, and I know I always will. I'd buried the desire to love so deeply inside me that it took a little time for me to recognise it. It crept up on me unawares, or rather— you did. You made yourself such a part of my life that I found I was breaking all the rules I'd made about relationships. I think I knew it for certain when I found myself wanting to stand up in front of a church-load of people and make you my wife.'

'Then why the hell didn't you tell me?' she asked him gently.

'Because I wasn't sure that you weren't still in love with Bob.'

She was crying now, bitterly regretting the barriers they had both erected around their hearts, and he caught her swiftly against his broad chest.

'Don't, Sam,' he pleaded, and his voice broke. 'Please don't cry, my darling.' And then he whispered against the soft fall of her hair, 'Is it too late for us, Sam? Can we start all over again?'

She pushed away from him, the tears already drying on her cheeks, an expression midway between incredulity and bemusement on her face. 'If you think that I'm ever going to spend a moment away from you again, then you're crazy!' she whispered.

'Crazy about you,' he growled, and he bent his head to kiss her with such sweet passion that she gave a little cry of disbelief.

It was some minutes before he raised his head and Sam looked up at him. 'I chucked my job in yesterday.'

'Was it awful?'

'Dreadful. The boss was a nightmare.'

'Worse than me?' he teased.

She put her head to one side and pretended to consider this. 'That's a tricky one—ouch!' As he nibbled her earlobe punishingly. She pulled away from him. 'Do you have problems working with me? I mean—*really*?'

He shook his head. 'Nope.'

'Then—can I come back again, as your assistant?'

'No,' he said gravely.

Sam swallowed. 'But——'

'You're not going to be an assistant any more,' he told her. 'You're going to have one of your own.'

'I don't understand.'

'You're far too good to be an assistant. From now on we're equal partners—not just at home but in the business, too. You can do as much of the advertising work as you like—all of it, if you want—while I concentrate on taking the kind of pictures I really want to take. And now——' his eyes narrowed with meaningful intent '—bed.'

Her mouth dried and her heart raced as he ran an idle finger from throat to nipple. 'But it's awfully early, isn't it?' she whispered, unable to keep a note of hungry amusement out of her voice.

'Yes,' he drawled. 'Just think. We've got the whole day ahead of us.'

As she lifted her head to kiss the hollow of his neck, he made a small sound of pleasure at the back of his throat, before picking her up and carrying her into the bedroom, and laying her down on the bed.

'Oh, Declan,' she sighed, as he began to unbutton her shirt, deliciously exposing the heated flesh of her breasts in the cream lace bra. His fingers unclasped the frontal clip and they spilled out into reverential hands.

He finished undressing her until she lay unashamedly offering her naked body for his delectation, revelling in the possessive gleam she read in his eyes.

He sat on the edge of the bed, very quiet and watchful. 'Samantha,' he said, very softly.

Her eyelids, which had been slowly closing in dreamy expectation, flew open in question at this use of her full name.

'Once,' he whispered, 'you told me that you were no Samantha, that Samanthas were beautiful and graceful. But let me tell you, my darling, that at this moment you're all Samantha—and you always have been to me. I could always——' he traced the outline of her trembling mouth with his finger '—call you that in future?'

'I think I prefer Sam,' she answered shakily. 'It's short and snappy.'

'Like you,' he teased, then groaned as she tugged at the buckle of his belt. She trickled the fingers of her other hand down over his chest, and beyond, her body alight with sensual delight at the freedom to touch him without restraint, with total love.

'Declan?'

'Mmm?'

'About that church wedding?'

'Mmm?'

'Is that still a possibility?'

He grinned, his eyes darkening with devilment, desire and pure love. 'Sam, darling?'

'What?'

'Just come here and kiss me.'

They were married in church three weeks later, with the choir's heavenly song soaring sweetly over their heads, while tall white candles guttered and the scent of waxen lilies perfumed the air.

Sam's parents were there, but without Charlotte or Bob, much to Sam's relief.

Declan had shaken his head in disbelief when he'd seen the invitation list. 'I can't believe you're inviting your sister, after what she tried to do.'

Sam had given him a grave smile. 'I owe it to my relationship with Flora not to sever the ties between us completely. Besides, she's having a rough time, and I'm so happy that nothing could spoil it. Mother says she and Bob are giving it another go, for Flora's sake, and for the sake of the new baby.'

And Flora was a bridesmaid, beaming and beautiful in a pearl-white silk gown which matched Sam's own.

Michael and his fiancée were there, and John with Lucy—they had just got engaged themselves.

There were also countless friends of Declan's and a few ex-girlfriends, too, including Fran, the stunning redhead she'd seen him with that very first night. She managed to get Sam alone for a few moments at the reception.

She smiled a slanting smile, and raised her enchanting green eyes heavenwards. 'Well done,' she whispered. 'You've managed where everyone else has failed. I've never seen him looking so happy. Look after him.'

'Oh, she will,' came Declan's deep voice as he came up from behind, his arm encircling Sam's waist, and smiled down at his bride. 'I'll make sure of that.'

Gita and Robin had been invited, but had declined, and Sam had thought that it was probably for the best. She certainly wasn't naïve enough to think that she and Gita would ever become bosom buddies—there was too much water under the bridge for that. Charlotte was dif-

ferent; she was family, with the shared bond of their
past, and the potential of a shared future.

Although they'd already had one honeymoon, Declan
had insisted on a second, and had booked a three-week
cruise on a private yacht in the Caribbean.

Sam changed into a flame-coloured silk dress and
tossed her bouquet, which was deftly caught by Fran,
and, festooned in rice, rose-petals and confetti, they
drove away in an open-topped chauffeur-driven car.

Sam leaned her head against Declan's broad shoulder.

'Happy?' he murmured.

'Mmm. Blissfully. Not so sure about *everyone* there
today, though,' she said impishly.

'Oh?'

'There were a lot of women in the congregation who
looked as though they should be wearing black arm-
bands.'

'Ah!' he smiled. 'And did you mind?'

'Not a bit.' She nestled closer into the warmth of his
embrace. 'Because you gave me something you never
gave to anyone else.'

'Tell me what I gave you, my darling.'

She touched his cheek very gently. 'You gave me your
heart, Declan.'

SUMMER SPECIAL!

Four exciting new Romances for the price of three

Each Romance features British heroines and their encounters with dark and desirable Mediterranean men. *Plus, a free Elmlea recipe booklet inside every pack.*

So sit back and enjoy your sumptuous summer reading pack and indulge yourself with the free Elmlea recipe ideas.

Available July 1994   Price £5.70

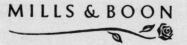

Accept 4 FREE Romances and 2 FREE gifts

FROM READER SERVICE

Here's an irresistible invitation from Mills & Boon. Please accept our offer of 4 FREE Romances, a CUDDLY TEDDY and a special MYSTERY GIFT! Then, if you choose, go on to enjoy 6 captivating Romances every month for just £1.90 each, postage and packing FREE. Plus our FREE Newsletter with author news, competitions and much more.

Send the coupon below to: Mills & Boon Reader Service, FREEPOST, PO Box 236, Croydon, Surrey CR9 9EL.

Yes! Please rush me 4 FREE Romances and 2 FREE gifts! Please also reserve me a Reader Service subscription. If I decide to subscribe I can look forward to receiving 6 brand new Romances for just £11.40 each month, post and packing FREE. If I decide not to subscribe I shall write to you within 10 days - I can keep the free books and gifts whatever I choose. I may cancel or suspend my subscription at any time. I am over 18 years of age.

Ms/Mrs/Miss/Mr _____ EP70R

Address _____

_____

Postcode _____ Signature _____